D0500212
PREUSS S
3348000121364Z
ANDALITE'S GIFT FIC APP
Applegate, K. A.

DATE DUE

MR 22 '02			
AP 23 '02			
MY 06 '02			
JY 01 '02			
JA 29 '03			
AP 7 '03			
OC 28 '03			
SE 23 '09			
AP 27 '10			
MAY 16 2017			
MAY 29 2017			

PERMA-BOUND®

The Andalite's Gift

Look for other ANIMORPHS®
titles by K.A. Applegate:

#1 The Invasion
#2 The Visitor
#3 The Encounter
#4 The Message
#5 The Predator
#6 The Capture
#7 The Stranger
#8 The Alien
#9 The Secret
#10 The Android
#11 The Forgotten
#12 The Reaction
#13 The Change
#14 The Unknown
#15 The Escape
#16 The Warning
#17 The Underground

<MEGAMORPHS>
#1 The Andalite's Gift

the andalite chronicles

ANIMORPHS®

<MEGAMORPHS #1>

The Andalite's Gift

K.A. Applegate

AN
APPLE
PAPERBACK

SCHOLASTIC INC.
New York Toronto London Auckland Sydney

Cover illustration by David B. Mattingly

If you purchased this book without a cover, you should be aware that this book is stolen property. It was reported as "unsold and destroyed" to the publisher, and neither the author nor the publisher has received any payment for this "stripped book."

No part of this publication may be reproduced in whole or in part, or stored in a retrieval system, or transmitted in any form or by any means, electronic, mechanical, photocopying, recording, or otherwise, without written permission of the publisher. For information regarding permission, write to Scholastic Inc., 555 Broadway, New York, NY 10012.

ISBN 0-590-21304-0

Copyright © 1997 by Katherine Applegate.
All rights reserved. Published by Scholastic Inc.
ANIMORPHS, APPLE PAPERBACKS, SCHOLASTIC, and associated logos are trademarks and/or registered trademarks of Scholastic Inc.

12 11 10 9/9 0 1 2/0

Printed in the U.S.A. 40

First Scholastic printing, June 1997

For Jean Feiwel, Craig Walker, and
Tonya Alicia Martin,
who morph my scribbles into books.

And, as always, for Michael

CHAPTER 1

Jake

My name is Jake. Just Jake. No last name. Or at least no last name I can tell you.

I am an Animorph. I guess that makes me one of the most hunted, endangered species on Earth. The Yeerks want me dead. They want my friends dead. So if they knew who I was, and how to find me, I wouldn't have a chance.

That's why I won't tell you my last name. And I won't tell you what city or state I live in. Because I want to go on living. I want to go on living so I can go on fighting *them*.

Are you one of those people who looks up at the night sky and wonders whether there is life out there among the stars? Do you wonder about

UFO's? Do you wonder whether aliens will ever come to Earth?

Well, stop wondering. The Yeerks are here.

They're a species of parasites — just little slugs, really. Little slugs that crawl inside your head and wrap themselves around your brain and make you do whatever they want you to do.

When that happens you stop being a true human being. You become a Controller. That's what we call a human who is under the control of a Yeerk. When you talk to a Controller, you may be looking at a human face, you may hear a human voice, but what you're really talking to is a Yeerk.

And they are everywhere. If you think you haven't seen one, you're wrong. The policeman in his patrol car, the clerk at the grocery store, your teacher, your pastor, your doctor: Any of them might be a Controller. Your mother, father, sister, or best friend: They could all be Controllers.

I know. My brother Tom is one of them. They have taken my brother from me and made him an enemy. I sit at the breakfast table every morning and make small talk, knowing all the while that Tom is not Tom anymore.

And they have taken my best friend's mother. Everyone thinks Marco's mother is dead. Only he and I know the truth: She, too, is one of *them*.

They are everywhere. They can be anyone.

They tear lives apart. They do unspeakable things. And we stand against them alone. Only we know the threat. We six: five Animorphs and one Andalite.

Five human kids with the power to become any animal we can touch. And a kid from another planet who looks like some weird mix of deer, human, and scorpion.

The six of us against all the might of the Yeerks, and all the evil genius of their leader, Visser Three.

Which is why Rachel was worried about leaving, even for a weekend.

We were all together that Friday evening — Marco, Cassie, Tobias, Rachel, and me. Ax wasn't there because he would have had to change into his human morph. He doesn't like to become human. I think he feels naked without his deadly tail.

So it was just the five of us in Cassie's barn, surrounded by all the chattering, snuffling, chirping, preening (and smelly) animals in their cages. The barn is also the Wildlife Rehabilitation Center. Cassie's parents are veterinarians. They use their barn to take in sick or injured wild animals.

"It's just this stupid, two-day gymnastics camp I signed up for a long time ago," Rachel was saying. "It's no big deal. It's something I was going to do back . . . you know, *before*."

"Rachel, you should go," Cassie said. "Our entire lives cannot be about fighting the Yeerks. We have to try to be seminormal. I mean, it can't all be danger and battle and fear, right? So go. But for now, help me lift up this crow's cage. He's going up on that shelf."

Cassie was trying to get us to help clean up the barn. We used the barn to get together. It was one of the few places we could meet with Tobias. See, he can't exactly go to the mall.

<Crows,> Tobias said, in thought-speak that we heard only in our minds. <I can't believe you're saving a crow. I hate crows. You know how he probably got that broken wing? Trying to mob a respectable hawk, that's how. Crows are total punks.>

Tobias was perched high in the rafters of the barn. From up there he could fly in and out through the hayloft. Tobias is a red-tailed hawk. Actually, in his mind, in his soul, he's human. But the power to morph has a terrifying downside. Stay in morph for more than two hours, and you stay forever. Tobias was trapped forever in a body with long, powerful wings, ripping, taloned feet, and fierce, angry eyes that stared at you around his hooked beak.

You would never guess that he had once been such a gentle guy. I guess he still is that guy. But he's also a hawk.

<Yeah, I'm looking at *you*, crow,> Tobias said in mock threat. Obviously, the crow did not understand thought-speak.

Cassie smiled. "Tobias, I promise when we release this guy, we'll take him far from your territory."

"I already told Melissa Chapman I wasn't going," Rachel said, going back to her own topic. "She went up to the camp this afternoon, right after school."

Marco, who had been lying back on a big bale of hay and staring at the ceiling, sat up. "Rachel doesn't think we can survive without her for two days. After all, she's the mighty *Xena: Warrior Princess.*"

It was Marco's teasing name for Rachel. Rachel has a tendency to be very bold. Anytime there's something borderline-insane that needs to be done, Rachel is always the first volunteer.

"Marco? You have hay stuck in your hair," Rachel said.

He ignored her remark. "Rachel thinks if she's not here and we have trouble, we'll all just run screaming and yammering like a bunch of scared little kids." He put on a phony-serious expression. "All I want to know is this: Why don't you dress like Xena? I mean, the whole leather and sword thing would really work for you."

"Okay, shut up, I'll go," Rachel said. "I'll go.

I'm going. Just to get away from Marco for a couple days. I'll catch the bus tomorrow morning."

"Think of me when you're on the uneven parallel bars," Marco said.

But it wasn't to Marco that Rachel looked. It was to Tobias. "You guys *will* stay out of trouble while I'm gone, won't you?"

<We'll be fine, Rachel,> Tobias said.

I saw Cassie smile, and my gaze met hers. She gave a slight nod. Cassie has a theory that Rachel and Tobias like each other. Not that Rachel has ever said anything, even though Rachel and Cassie are best friends. Cassie thinks it's sweet and romantic. I just think it's kind of sad. I mean, as far as we know, Tobias will never be fully human again.

"We should all just enjoy a nice, normal weekend," I said. "Have normal fun. We've had plenty of danger and excitement."

Marco sent me a sly, resentful look. "*Some* of us are going to have more fun than some others. *Some* of us are going to pool parties that *some* of us were not invited to." He shook his fists melodramatically at the ceiling. "Why? Why? What does that girl have against me?"

I rolled my eyes. "Here we go again."

Cassie rescued me. "I need someone strong to come outside with me, help me carry in some new cages from the truck. Marco?"

"Oh! My back!" Marco cried. "A sudden, shooting pain."

"I'm coming, Cassie," I said. I gave Marco a shove, pushing him back on his bale of hay. "You are so pathetic."

"Don't strain yourself," Marco said with a cocky grin.

Outside, out of the golden glow of the barn's lights, it was getting dark. A full moon had risen, and you could just see the first stars off to the east.

The pickup truck was piled precariously high with wire cages. I climbed up and began to untie the rope that held them in place.

"It seems strange — Rachel going away — even for a couple days," Cassie said. "And it seems even stranger that it would seem strange. I mean, it should be no big deal."

"Well, I guess when life turns completely crazy, it's the normal things that start to seem strange."

Cassie nodded slowly. For a while she said nothing. She just stood there with her arms crossed, looking up at the moon.

I climbed down off the truck. "What's bothering you?"

She shrugged. "Nothing. Just . . . a feeling. I don't know. Bad dreams, I guess."

"I have those, too," I said. "We all do. You

can't live through all this and not have it bother you. What's the dream about? The ant thing?"

We'd morphed ants once. We'd gone down into an ant tunnel and had been attacked by an enemy colony of ants. No one wanted to go through that, ever again. Not ever.

"No, not the ants," Cassie said. "At least not directly. It's . . . it's dumb. There's . . . something. I don't even know what it is. But it's not a good thing. And it asks me to make a choice. In the dream I have to decide who lives and who dies."

I moved closer to Cassie and put my arm around her shoulder. There were goose bumps on her bare arms.

"I never used to be afraid, Jake," Cassie said. "Not of anything. And now it's like I'm afraid all the time."

"You deal with it, though," I said. It made me nervous talking about feelings like this. I guess I think if you just don't talk about the fear, it will go away. "You always deal with it," I repeated.

"So far," Cassie said softly. "So far."

CHAPTER 2
Rachel

My name is Rachel. I live with my mom and my two little sisters. We live pretty close to Jake, who lives pretty close to Marco. Cassie is the farthest one out because she lives on a farm.

I guess we're a pretty average bunch of kids. I mean, we *were* a pretty average bunch. Marco lives with his dad. I live with my mom. Jake and Cassie each have both parents around. We go to school. We do homework. We hang at the mall. We listen to music. Go to movies on the weekend. Normal. Boringly average.

Until one night when we happened to hook up together at the mall and decided to take a shortcut through an abandoned construction site off the highway.

We weren't a "group" back then. Jake was my cousin, but we didn't really see each other, except at school. Cassie was my best friend, and had been for a long time. But Marco was just Jake's friend, not mine. And Tobias was this guy Jake felt sorry for because he came from such a messed-up home and got picked on by bullies.

That's Jake: When he sees some guy getting his head stuffed in a toilet at school, he is absolutely going to stop it. Jake isn't some big tough guy or anything. It's just that when he tells you, in that calm, reasonable voice of his, to stop picking on someone, you stop. You just do.

Jake is sort of the one in charge. It's not something he ever wanted. It just seems natural for him to take over.

Not that Jake is without his own level of stupidity. I mean, he was right there with us, walking through an isolated, abandoned construction site that night. Wasn't the smartest thing we ever did.

But the way it turned out, the real danger that night was not from some mad slasher. The real danger was from a totally unexpected direction.

See, that's where the damaged Andalite spaceship landed. Right there in the construction site. That's where we saw our first alien. That's where we learned about the Yeerk threat. And that's where the Andalite, Prince Elfangor, gave us our power to morph.

It's where Elfangor died, too. We watched it happen. We watched that brave, decent, kind creature be murdered by Visser Three. Murdered for trying to protect the people of Earth.

Anyway. That's when we became a group. It was Marco who came up with a name for what we were. *Animorphs*. Persons who can morph animals.

The Andalite left us the burden of fighting the Yeerks, and gave us that one weapon: the power to morph. Like all weapons, it has dangers even to those who use it for a good cause. Just ask Tobias.

But it is an awesome power. We have done some damage to the Yeerks. And to be honest with you, sometimes the morphing power is just plain fun. Right now, though, my "normal" life was calling.

It was already getting warm by the time I walked over to school the next morning. The bus to the camp was due to come at eleven. I got to school an hour early.

I stopped on the sidewalk in front of the school and checked my watch. The sun was climbing fast, and you could tell it was going to be a really hot day. I smiled. It would be a good day for flying.

I crossed the athletic field and headed for the woods behind the school. I wanted to check in with Tobias before I left. It's no big thing. It's just that I kind of take care of stuff Tobias needs. I bring him books sometimes. You know — things he can't get in the woods.

But Tobias isn't always an easy guy to find. Especially in the morning, when he's likely to be out hunting his breakfast. I knew I would need great eyes and speed to find him and still get back in time to catch the bus.

It's funny how it never even occurred to me that I was in a very dangerous position. See, my mom and my friends all thought I was heading to camp. They wouldn't expect to see me for a couple of days. But the camp people didn't think I was coming. So they wouldn't expect to see me, either.

But none of this occurred to me. After all, what did I have to worry about? Little did I know.

So, I entered the woods, put my outer clothing in my bag, hid it beneath some low-lying bushes, and took a quick look around to make sure I was alone. Then I began to morph.

I focused my mind on one of the many animals whose DNA is part of me.

Every morphing is unique. The changes never happen the same way twice. This time, the first thing to change was my mouth. My lips grew hard and stiff. And when I rolled my eyes downward, I could see my mouth become bright yellow and bulge outward.

As that happened, I began to shrink. The pine needle-covered ground came up toward me as I lost a foot of height within a few seconds. Then another foot.

The strangest thing, though, was my skin. The flesh on my bare arms began to melt like candle wax. It melted and ran together. It formed intricate patterns, like a tattoo of feathers. Suddenly, the painted feather patterns were no longer just designs. Actual feathers began to emerge.

The feathers were dark brown, except for the ones that replaced my blond hair and the skin of my face and neck. Those feathers were all snowy white.

By the time the morph was nearly complete, I only stood about two feet tall. My feet had split open and formed yellow talons, each of which ended in a wicked, hooked claw.

My arms rose up, horizontal. Long feathers sprouted from them, even as my solid, heavy, human bones became hollow and light.

It took just a few minutes for the transformation to be done. I was no longer human. I was a bald eagle.

I turned to face the breeze and opened my wings. They stretched six feet from tip to tip. I felt the wind press against my feathers, stretching my muscles. I flapped several times with great power, and then . . . I was airborne! I drew my talons up snug against my body.

I flapped and rose. I flapped more, and soared above the trees. The top branches reached for me but missed. I flapped still more and caught a good, strong headwind. It was like an invisible wedge that forced me up and up.

Up and up! I rose till I was several hundred feet above the treetops. I could see the school down below. I could see the bus parked in the empty lot. And, being an eagle, I could see a great deal more.

Looking through the eyes of an eagle is like having built-in binoculars. From hundreds of feet in the air I could see field mice just poking their noses out of their holes. I could see ants crawling up the trunks of trees. I could look down through the water of a stream and see the tiny fish feeding there. I could see everything, like no human will ever see.

I turned toward the deeper woods where Tobias lived.

Maybe there is something better than flying free, high above the trees, riding the wind, but I doubt it. It was freedom beyond any dream of freedom. I loved it. For all the pain that has come from the war with the Yeerks, I swear sometimes just being able to fly makes it all worthwhile.

I was close to Tobias's territory when I spotted something interesting below me. It was a deer-like animal, running swiftly through the trees. When I focused my laser-intensity eagle sight, I could see the semihuman torso and face and the deadly scorpion tail.

Ax! Or, Aximili-Esgarrouth-Isthill, to use his complete name. Ax is an Andalite. The only Andalite to survive a terrible space battle with the Yeerks. Prince Elfangor was his brother.

It was fun watching him run. I've never seen anything that can look as delicate and cute one minute — and as dangerous the next — as an Andalite.

I decided to swoop down over Ax and say hi. I spilled a little air from my wings and dropped, thrilled by the feeling of a controlled fall from hundreds of feet up. It's like jumping off a sky-scraper, knowing you can survive.

I dropped toward the trees.

I actually had time to notice the nest in a high branch. Just out of the corner of my eye. I had time to think, *Isn't that cute? Baby birds.*

And then they hit me.

SWOOP!

SWOOP!

Faster than me! More agile! Small, dark birds zipped straight at me like they were going to hit. Too many of them!

SWOOP! SWOOP! SWOOP!

I turned a hard left. In a flash I knew what was happening. They thought I was attacking their nest. They were "mobbing" me! Trying to drive me off.

I banked a hard turn. Too fast! I was still going fast from the dive. Too fast! Bank left! Turn!

WHAM!

I barely saw the tree trunk before I hit. Headfirst.

Down I fell. Down through branches that tore at me, banged me, slapped me, ripped at my feathers.

I hit the ground hard. I was hurt. I knew I was hurt. Fading out. My mind was swimming. Human thoughts . . . eagle instinct, all swirling, shifting. I was falling down, down a dark well.

Down . . .

Morph out, I told myself. *Rachel . . . MORPH OUT!*

And then I was gone.

CHAPTER 3
Marco

"Look, it's simple," I explained patiently. "There's this party. This *pool* party. And I was not invited. Not only was I not invited, but the girl who's having the party went out of her way to *not* invite me."

By the way, hi, my name is Marco. I'm an Animorph, too. I'm the smart, cute one. No, seriously. Jake is the bossy one, Cassie's the nice one, Rachel is the stupidly brave one, and Tobias is a bird.

I am the cute one. All the girls think so. All except Darlene.

<So you are not wanted at this party. But you want to go, anyway?>

That was Ax speaking. Well, not exactly

"speaking." He's an Andalite, and Andalites don't have mouths. They do "thought-speak." It's like telepathy. We can all do it when we're in a morph. But for Andalites it's their normal language. Ax's real name is Aximili-Esgarrouth-Isthill. Rolls right off the tongue, doesn't it? Now you know why we just call him Ax.

"That's right," I explained to him. "I mean, Jake and Cassie were both invited. Rachel was invited, but she's going to that stupid gymnastics thing. Basically, everyone at school was invited. All I'm saying is, there must be a reason why I was not invited. And I think I know what that reason is: Darlene likes me. There's *no* other possible explanation."

Ax looked puzzled. <Is that common among humans? Do you avoid the ones you like?>

"Not like. *Like*. I like you, Ax. But I don't *like* you. There's like, and then there's like, *like*."

Ax stared at me with his main eyes. He has four eyes altogether. Two of them are fairly normal. The other two eyes are on these stalklike things that stick out of the top of his head like those little horns a giraffe has. On the end of each stalk, he has an eye, which he can point in any direction. Very weird. But you can't sneak up on the guy, that's for sure.

<I am confused,> Ax said.

"It's okay. You don't need to understand. I just want you to go with me."

<To the party?>

"That's right. We have to go to the party to see what Darlene says about me. She and her cheerleader friends are probably going to talk about me. I want to hear what they say."

<And you want me to go with you?>

"Yeah. You and me. I need someone to watch my back."

<But Prince Jake will be at the party, won't he?>

I rolled my eyes. Ax is convinced Jake is his prince. I guess Andalites are into the whole royalty thing.

"Yes, Jake will be there. But Jake is not going to help me spy on Darlene, is he? Neither will Cassie. Cassie doesn't exactly fit in with the cheerleader crowd. They talk about clothes and guys. Cassie talks about animals and saving the world or whatever."

<Pardon me if I sound skeptical, and please don't be offended,> Ax said, <but I sense that maybe this is a dishonorable idea.>

<You sense right, Ax.>

Tobias. He zipped swiftly overhead and landed on a low branch. He was carrying something in his beak.

"Hi, Tobias," I said. "Do you have it?"

<Yes. And do you know how hard it is to fly around with a live, squirming mouse in my beak?>

"Drop it down to me," I said.

<You are a twisted, devious human being, Marco,> Tobias said. <Ax, if you have any sense you won't get involved in this.>

<Tobias, I am suffering. I have small, itching bumps on parts of my body. Marco has agreed to help me, if I will help him. He has a rare medicine that will help.>

<Marco, you're blackmailing Ax with flea powder? Ax, my friend, you just picked up a couple fleas. It's normal in the woods. Don't let Marco jerk you —>

"Just give me the mouse and stop acting like a parent," I interrupted. "I'm not blackmailing anyone. I'll bring Ax the flea powder. Jeez. The suspicion around here."

Tobias dropped the mouse and I caught it with one hand. It squirmed and I almost dropped it. But as I began to "acquire" it, it calmed down.

See, if you want to morph into an animal, you have to acquire it first. You have to make contact. Then you sort of focus on it, concentrate on it. The animal goes into a trance. And meanwhile the animal's DNA is being absorbed.

Don't ask me how it works. It's some weird Andalite biotechnology. I just know it works.

When I was done acquiring the mouse I handed it to Ax. He had to use both hands to hold on. Andalite arms and hands are kind of puny. Of course, they also have four legs, and those are pretty strong. I mean, Ax can haul when he wants to. I'll bet he could do forty miles an hour.

Then there's that tail. The tail is the reason Andalites will never be considered truly "cute." I've seen Ax use his tail on full-grown Hork-Bajir warriors. And fast? Man, you don't even see it move. It's like WHAPP! and all of a sudden a Hork-Bajir only has one arm. I believe Ax could chop down a tree with that tail if he felt like it.

<Marco, you know Jake will roast you alive behind this,> Tobias said. <Morphing for personal reasons?>

"Hey, Jake was invited to the party, all right? *He'll* be soaking up the rays at poolside. *He'll* be having a good time. Meanwhile I, his best friend, was not even invited. Jake is big on justice. I ask you: Is this justice? No. Clearly not."

<Marco, Jake says the last time you were invited to one of Darlene's pool parties you floated a Baby Ruth bar in the pool and told everyone it was . . . you know. Maybe that's why you weren't invited.>

"I was like six years old," I protested. "I didn't know any better. Besides, it was funny."

<Marco, you were not six. You were ten.>

"Whatever. Who remembers this stuff?"

<Darlene does.>

I ignored Tobias. "Are you done acquiring the mouse?" I asked Ax. "If so, give him back to Tobias for lunch."

<I've eaten, thanks,> Tobias said. <But you shouldn't laugh. You want to go play mouse, you better remember something: There are a lot of predators who enjoy eating mice. It's a dangerous world out there.>

"And who would know that better than you, Mr. Predator?"

Tobias laughed. <Even we predators get ours sometimes. I saw a bald eagle get mobbed by a bunch of jays this morning. Slammed into a tree. I guess the eagle was going after their nest.>

"There won't be any eagles at the party," I said. "The bird world is your problem, dude. I have a party to attend."

<Darlene likes him,> Ax said. <But she doesn't *like* him.>

<That's pretty much how everyone feels about Marco,> Tobias said with a laugh.

CHAPTER 4
Jake

"I feel bad even going to this party," I said. "Darlene should have invited Marco. He wouldn't have done the Baby Ruth thing again. He's much more mature now. Sort of."

"I feel a little guilty, too," Cassie said. She lowered her voice to a whisper and put her mouth close to my ear. "But I seem to remember you saying we should all take the weekend off and be normal. So I am going to be normal."

We were both in our swim suits, sitting in those long pool chairs. You know — the ones you can adjust so you're lying down or sitting up.

There were forty or fifty kids around the pool. Darlene's family has money, I guess, because it's a very nice pool.

There was a long table loaded up with chips and dip and cold cuts. And there were coolers full of iced soft drinks. There was decent rock music playing on the stereo. Some kids were dancing.

It wasn't even noon yet, but the sun was already bright. It was going to be hot, that was for sure. I almost envied Rachel heading up to the mountains. It would probably be cooler up there.

"It feels weird to just sit around and relax," I said.

As soon as the words were out of my mouth, I heard a bloodcurdling scream.

"Yaaaaaaahhh!" someone shrieked.

"Oh! Oh! Oh! Oh!" someone else cried.

I sat straight up. Trouble! I could feel the familiar rush of adrenaline. I quickly looked around, checking for the ways to escape, the places where we could stand and fight, the places we might be able to hide for a quick morph. People were running.

No . . . on a closer look, only a couple of girls were running. They were the ones screaming.

"That's Darlene," Cassie said. She sent me a puzzled, worried look.

"Oh! Oh! Oh! Get it away from me!" Darlene screamed. "Get it awaaaaay!"

Darlene ran straight toward us. She ran like the hounds of hell were right behind her. "Help me!" she screamed. "It's after me!"

"What is it?!" I yelled to no one in particular.

"Mice!" this girl named Tracy yelled. "Miiiice!"

Then I spotted them: two tiny, harmless little mice. Two little mice, chasing Darlene like a pair of lions trying to bring down a buffalo.

Darlene dodged right. The mice went right after her. And then something very interesting happened. This guy named Hans yelled, "Darlene! Run this way! I'll stomp them!"

Darlene headed for Hans. Hans raised his foot up, ready to stomp the mice as they shot past. But suddenly the mice turned a sharp left, shot around behind Hans, and tore off after Darlene again.

Right then, I knew. The mice had heard Hans's plan. They had dodged away to safety.

"Real mice don't chase people," Cassie said, giving me a meaningful look.

"No, they don't," I agreed.

"Marco," Cassie whispered. "And he must have dragged Ax into it, too."

"I'll kill him," I said. "Just as soon as we save him."

I raced around the pool. I tore through a mess of overturned chairs and soda cans and paper plates. Cassie went the other way.

"Help me! Help me!" Darlene screamed, running toward the patio door.

"Hey!" Cassie yelled as loudly as she could. "It's just a couple of mice. Nothing to be afraid of."

One of the mice hesitated. Marco had recognized Cassie's voice.

"You know, if those mice want to live, they should go to Cassie," I said, trying to sound like I was making a joke. "Otherwise, someone might *kill* them." Then, under my breath, I added, "Someone like me."

<I heard that,> Marco said to me in thought-speak.

I could hear his thought-speak. But since I was not in a morph, I could not reply. Probably a good thing. I might have used some words I shouldn't use.

It was total pandemonium! Forty kids running around like idiots. Half running away from the mice. Half running after the mice. Everyone making lots of noise.

"Come here, little mice," Cassie said loudly.

We were trying to make Marco realize he had to head for Cassie. I knew he could hear us — mice have excellent hearing.

But Marco either didn't get it, or had decided he wasn't done chasing Darlene.

"Aaaaahhh!" Darlene was not done screaming, either. She reached the patio door. She was still screaming as she disappeared inside her house.

Marco was after her like a shot, with Ax right behind.

<Don't worry,> I heard Marco say in thought-speak a few seconds later. <We're down in the basement. We're demorphing. Just make sure no one comes down to the basement looking for mice.>

"Oh, man," I muttered. I ran for the patio door.

THUMP!

I slammed hard into Hans, and both of us went rolling. No less than eight other people slammed into us, one right after another. It was like some bad football game, all of us jumbled together, yelling and giggling and pushing and trying to untangle our legs and arms.

As it turned out, that pileup saved my life.

I sucked wind and tried to stand up, and the sky above us grew dark.

It was so sudden and so complete that everyone just froze.

I looked up. The sun was hidden behind a swirling cloud of dust. Like a flat tornado. A tornado in a clear sky.

I felt a terrible sensation of dread from deep down inside.

The dust swarm grew solid.

Within seconds, it assumed a shape.

A shape like nothing ever seen on planet Earth.

And then it struck.

CHAPTER 5
Marco

Okay. *Okay*, maybe it was a little immature to sneak into Darlene's party as a mouse. But you didn't hear what she said about me!

Me and Ax morphed in a vacant lot a block away. Then we toddled on over on our little mouse legs to the party.

Of course, first we had to get used to the mouse morph. See, when you morph you don't just get the animal's body. You get its brain, too. And most animal brains are loaded with different instincts. Usually hunger. Also fear.

The mouse had a lot of each. He was very obsessed about food. And he was one scared little animal. It's often that way when you first morph a new species. As soon as Ax and I achieved total mousehood, those instincts kicked in big time.

RUN! RUN! RUN! RUN!

The mouse didn't like being out in the open, in broad daylight. He was scared of predators. Seriously scared.

RUN! RUN! RUN! RUN!

So we ran. It was like one minute you're a normal human thinking, *Hmmm, isn't it fascinating shrinking down like this, growing a tail, having big whiskers?* And the next minute that mouse brain kicks in and suddenly you are charged up with the energy of a thousand cups of coffee on top of a thousand bowls of Captain Crunch, and you are ENERGIZED!

<I can't control this creature!> Ax wailed. <It's insane!>

<Just go with it,> I said. <It'll chill out eventually.>

Let me tell you: Mice can move on those little legs. It was like being strapped to the front bumper of an Indy 500 car.

ZOOOOM!

We hauled butt, zipping in wild terror over leaves of grass as big as trees, pieces of gravel the size of beach balls, and bugs the size of collies. That much I'm used to. I've morphed small animals before.

But what was sick was that I really, really wanted to stop and eat some of those bugs. There was this one beetle, kind of bluish-black, and the mouse brain was like, *Ah, cool, lunch!*

But it was more terrified than it was hungry, so we just kept running like out-of-control lunatics, and I missed out on the flavor of bug. Eventually, we were able to get some control.

<Ax. You okay, man?> I called to him in thought-speak.

<I am fine. But these mice have very powerful instincts.>

<Yeah. Scared little things, aren't they?>

<Animals develop instincts for a good reason,> Ax said darkly. <If the mouse is cautious, it probably has good reasons.>

<Well, if we see any cats, we'll just morph back,> I said.

<Yes. If we live long enough.>

In any case, we toddled off to the party, two little mice looking for a good time.

Mouse senses are excellent, fortunately. Hearing is great. The sense of smell is great. The eyes are decent, but it's hard to see much when you're only an inch tall and your face is down at dirt level.

Still, I was able to locate Darlene by the sound of her voice. She was talking to her friends about the usual stuff: school, music, some cute guy on TV. Ax and I hid underneath Darlene's chair, so I was able to hear everything pretty well.

All I could see of Darlene was this enormous chair roof over my head — stretched bands of interwoven plastic, bulging down like they might burst and crush me. Quite a distance away I could see her legs, looking like two gigantic pink pillars.

<Well, this is boring,> I said to Ax.

<What did you expect?>

<I expected them to be talking about me, naturally,> I said. Then it occurred to me. I could thought-speak to Darlene! I would just say the word "Marco" in her head. She wouldn't know where it had come from. She'd probably think someone had said it aloud. With thought-speak, you can either do it so everyone hears you, or sort of aim it at just one person.

<Marco,> I said.

"What?" Darlene asked. "What *about* Marco?"

"Nothing about Marco," this girl named Kara said.

"Good, because I don't even want his name mentioned at my party. He's such a jerk. I mean, after what he did? Throwing Baby Ruth bars in my pool? Panicking everybody?"

"He's so immature," a girl named Ellen said.

"No duh," Darlene said. "He thinks he's so cool and so cute, but he's totally *not*. He always makes jokes about stuff that aren't even funny."

Well. I could stand them saying I was immature. That's what girls always say. But saying I wasn't funny?

I would show them funny. Oh, yes.

I took off. I ran for the legs. Ax came after me yelling, <What are we doing?!>

<We're just going to see how good Darlene's sense of humor is,> I yelled back. I ran for that big pink leg. I saw the foot pressing heavily down on the grass. I shot past her heel, which was like a wall to me, and aimed for the toes.

Let me just say this: Darlene thinks she's perfect in every way. But her toenails definitely needed trimming.

I scampered right onto her foot. I zoomed across her foot, then scrabbled wildly around her ankle and back over her toes.

<Yee-HAH!> I crowed to Ax. <That'll give her something else to complain about!>

"Oh! Oh! Ohhhhhhhhh!" Darlene screamed.

Up flew the foot! I jumped off just in time. And then she was outta there, screaming and yammering like a total ninny.

Naturally, I chased her. And naturally, Ax came with me.

It was total, absolute fun! I'm sorry, I know it was wrong and all, but man, it was so cool.

That is, until I heard Hans yelling about how he was going to stomp me. That would never do.

I did not intend to be stomped by Hans's big stinky foot.

I heard Jake's big voice yelling. And Cassie's sweeter — but still annoyed — voice.

<Oh, man. It's Jake,> I said to Ax. <Busted.>

I raced for cover, looking for a place to morph back to human. Big stomping feet were landing all around me. They were slow, but man, they were big. Everyone was totally overreacting. I mean, give me a break, I was two inches long! How scary could I possibly be?

Then it occurred to me. The house! We could run inside, race down to the basement where no one would be, morph back real fast, and then . . . Well, and then there I would be, just me and an Andalite. Great. That wouldn't look too strange.

<Ax! Stay with me. We need to demorph. Then you have to do your human morph real quick, okay?>

<I have the feeling, Marco, that this was not a good idea.>

<Nah. Everything according to plan.>

ZOOM! Over the threshold onto the patio! ZOOM! Into the house itself! ZOOM! Past a hysterical Darlene, who was on the couch with a pillow over her head.

ZOOM! Along carpet till we hit linoleum.

Suddenly, the scent of dark places. Mouse places! Yes, it was going to work!

We ran across a step and leapt, falling . . . falling . . . PLOP! to land on the next step. Again and again, step after step, at a speed that felt like we were flying rockets.

It was so cool! If you overlooked the fact that it was maybe slightly stupid.

<Don't worry,> I called to Jake in thought-speak. <We're in the basement. We're going to demorph. Just make sure no one comes down to the basement looking for mice.>

We lost our pursuers. No one followed us down the steps. And even as I ran, I started to demorph.

I was halfway back to human, a strange mix of mouse tail and huge ears and human legs — a scary-looking creature. The way Mickey Mouse would look if he'd been invented by Stephen King. Ax looked even worse, half-mouse, half-Andalite.

Just as I was thinking, *Hey, this will all be fine,* the entire world just flew apart.

Crrrrr-RUNCH!

Sunlight streamed down! The entire roof had been ripped away! The entire roof!

Wood and beams and concrete just shattered and ripped and fell in huge chunks. I couldn't even make sense of it. I mean, the entire world around me was just being shredded. Shredded, like the universe was being run through a food processor.

Then I saw it. It was gigantic! Enormous! A creature that seemed to be made of nothing but teeth and blades and destruction. It was like twenty Hork-Bajir glued together and given dragon wings.

B-R-R-A-A-A-K!

It was ripping the house apart with unbelievable power.

The noise was terrifying. The scream of ripping wood. The shattering crunch of concrete being torn up — just torn up, like it was nothing! Pipes bending. Wires sizzling and popping as they exploded into showers of sparks.

"Look out!" I yelled to Ax with my now-human voice. Beams were falling around us. Splinters were flying through the air.

I barely noticed that I had finished morphing. I was human again. Somehow Ax had kept his concentration and was fully in his human morph.

We were defenseless. Two kids without a weapon between us.

Above our heads, where there had been a house just seconds before, the beast hovered in the sun.

It looked down at us with a dozen weird eyes that seemed to be stuck here and there at random. It stared at us the way I'd seen Tobias stare at his prey.

It was going to destroy us. There was no question in my mind. And no question that it could.

"Oh, man," I moaned. "I don't like this."

Then . . . the eyes all flickered at once. The beast seemed uncertain.

And to my utter relief and utter amazement, the thing began to disperse. He became dust again. Just a cloud of dust that thinned and disappeared.

I was shaking so badly I couldn't stand up. But I was alive.

CHAPTER 6

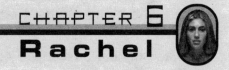

Rachel

I woke up.

I was on my back, lying on a bed of pine needles and crispy dried leaves. I was staring up at trees. The sun shone through the branches.

My first thought was, *What am I doing here?*

I had no idea how I had gotten to these woods. Or even what woods these were.

"What am I doing here?" I started to say out loud. But the words were garbled, mangled. They were more of a screech than actual words.

I felt a tingle of fear.

What was going on? What was going *on*? Why was I here? Why couldn't I talk?

I shouldn't be here. I should be . . . where?

Where should I be? I tried to concentrate. How had I come here? Where was I *before*? Where . . . where did I belong?

But nothing came. Nothing! I couldn't remember how I'd gotten there. I couldn't remember where I had been. Ever.

Suddenly, it hit me in a wave of dread that made my heart skip several beats: I didn't know who I was. I did not know my own *name*.

I tried to sit up. And that's when I saw.

"Aaaaaaahhhhhh!" I screamed in a weird, high-pitched shriek.

My legs . . . they were encased in a black leotard. And I could see that the upper half of each leg was shaped like a normal human leg. But the end . . . the bottom half suddenly changed shape. And from the bottom of the leotard, huge talons appeared.

I looked at my hand. Five fingers. Five human fingers, but they sprouted with feathers. There were feathers sticking out of my flesh!

I felt my face. Skin. Skin on my cheeks and my neck. But then, my bristling, feathered fingers felt my mouth.

It was a beak! A hard, tearing beak.

It was a nightmare! That was it, I was having a nightmare! I had to wake up. I had to get out of this dream.

"Aaaaahhhhh!" I screamed again. And the unhuman sound of my own voice frightened me still more.

I had to control the panic. I had to. I had to. But my legs! My face! My hands!

Don't panic, I ordered myself. *You will not panic. You will not panic! This isn't real.*

And yet I could feel the pine needles beneath me. And the warmth of the sun as it lanced through the branches. It all *felt* real.

Was this how I always was? Was I some sort of freak? Half-bird, half-human?

No. I knew that was wrong. And I knew that people did not become birds. And yet here I was, with feathers and a beak, and no memory of who I was. I looked like some horrible creature who was halfway through changing from bird to human — or the other way around.

Was that it? Had I been in the process of changing from one to the other? And which one was I really? Who was I? *What* was I?

Come on, I ordered myself. *Get a grip. Get a grip.*

But I could feel screams boiling up inside me. I could scream and scream and scream.

No. No. Start that and you may never stop, I thought. *Use your head. Think.*

I strained to remember, but it was as if half

my brain were wrapped in a dense fog. I couldn't see through it. No matter how I tried.

You're a human, I told myself silently. *You're human, not a bird. And if you could change this far, maybe you can change more.*

I closed my eyes. I wanted to concentrate, and I did not want to see my body. Terror rattled through me, shaking my bones, churning my insides.

I was human. I wanted to be fully human. Human again.

Then . . . I began to feel changes. I opened my eyes. As I watched, the talons shriveled and split and became toes.

It was revolting to watch. It made me sick. But then I realized something. As soon as I lost concentration, the changes stopped. That had to be it! I must have been changing, and something had broken my concentration. I could not stay the way I was. I was a nightmare. I had to get out!

I felt a shadow over the sun. I thought it was a passing cloud. I couldn't let myself be distracted.

I focused down again. Human. I wanted to be human. I felt the feathers melt into my skin. I felt my beak become soft lips.

The sun was very dim now. Something was blocking it. I felt a chill. I looked up.

Just above the trees, a cloud of dust swirled wildly, like some flattened tornado. It swirled and concentrated.

A dust cloud. But not a dust cloud, really.

As I lay there, I had a terrible feeling. A feeling that this swirling, thickening cloud was watching me. Considering me. Focusing on me.

But I could *not* allow myself to be distracted. I was still not fully human. And I wanted to be human again. Maybe . . . maybe once I was human, I would remember who I was.

CHAPTER 7
Tobias

I have seen a lot of strange things since that first evening when we walked through the construction site where the Andalite prince had landed his damaged fighter.

Back then I was just a kid. A boy. A dork, I guess. It's getting hard to remember. But yeah, I guess I was a dweeb. I remember that I met Jake because he stepped in to save me from some punks who wanted to flush my head in the toilet.

Well, a lot has changed since then.

I've gotten so I can deal with being what I am now. I've accepted the fact that I am no longer completely human. But I'm not completely a hawk, either.

Like I said, I've seen strange things. But

nothing stranger than what I saw that morning as I floated in the high thermals, a mile above Darlene's house.

See, I was flying "cover." It's one of the ways I'm able to help my friends. Marco hadn't *asked* me to fly cover for his idiotic little escapade, but I figured I'd better. Besides, I'd already eaten. A small snake, an unusual delicacy for me. I had nothing else to do, really, but catch a thermal and ride it up.

A thermal is an updraft of warm air. You spread your wings and it lifts you up like an elevator. Once you're up, you can just float there forever. You barely have to flap your wings.

So I was up pretty high. High enough that I could see everything from the edge of the woods to the south, all the way to the center of the city a few miles away. But I stayed low enough that I could still watch Marco and Ax morph.

They ran around like fools till they got a grip on their mouse brains. Then, as they gained control, they set off purposefully toward Darlene's house.

Marco is an extremely smart guy. I don't know if Ax is smart for an Andalite, but he's really smart by human standards. Neither of them really understood how dangerous it is to be a mouse, walking openly across a suburban lawn in broad daylight.

I mean, you might as well just tie raw steaks to your legs and go for a walk with a wolf pack. Hawks kill mice. Cats kill mice. And let me tell you something: Two groups of animals you don't want chasing you are hawks and cats.

From the air I observed one fat tabby cat who spotted them passing by. But I guess he was full, or just feeling too lazy, lying out in the sun. The cat let them pass undisturbed.

I also spotted a Cooper's hawk checking them out. He was definitely thinking about mouse for lunch. I signaled the Cooper's that these were *my* prey and he backed off. Fortunately, I was bigger than he was, and he wasn't hungry enough to fight.

I watched as Marco and Ax reached Darlene's pool party. I relaxed then. If they didn't get stepped on, they'd probably be safe. Still, watching the party made me a little sad. The people seemed to be having a good time. Kids were splashing in the pool and running around and yelling and talking.

It was a whole different universe than the one I lived in. I had the other Animorphs and Ax for friends. But I didn't have friends like myself. Hawks don't get together and have parties. Mostly, when you see another hawk it means trouble, a fight for territory.

Down below, I saw Marco chasing some girl. *Good grief,* I thought. *Why am I not surprised?*

The girl ran inside the house. Marco and Ax ran after her, trailing a posse of guys, one of whom was clearly Jake.

Then I began to see something bizarre. A dust storm. That's what it looked like, anyway. Like one of those little dust devils that kick up out in the desert or prairie.

It swirled like a compact tornado. I was fascinated because wind is very important to me. Wind is life and death to me sometimes.

The tornado was getting tighter. More solid. I strained my hawk eyes to see every detail. I spilled air from my wings and swooped lower to get a better view.

And then . . . it wasn't a dust cloud anymore.

It was a creature! A beast made up of gnashing mouths and whirling blades.

It dived at the house, ripping it apart like it was made out of Legos. It seemed to be chewing its way through brick and wood and shingle. It was like watching a garbage disposal grind up a carrot.

Kids were screaming. They were running wildly, this way and that. Suddenly, half the house was gone. Just *gone*, and I could see straight down into the basement. Straight down at Marco, human once more, and Ax in his human morph.

I folded my wings back and dived like a rocket. Maybe I could distract the beast.

Then, for no apparent reason, the beast began to dissolve.

I pulled up sharply, still a few hundred feet up. I could see Marco practically faint from relief. Ax didn't look too happy, either. But they were both alive. And Jake and Cassie? Both were staring up at the sky in horror.

The dust beast dissolved into a cloud again. A human eye would not have seen anything after that. But I didn't have human eyes. I saw the dust cloud disperse. But I also saw the individual particles streaming away toward the forest.

The particles were moving at incredible speed. They were not being blown by the wind, I was sure of that.

They were moving all on their own. Very fast, toward the woods.

CHAPTER 8

Rachel

Human. Be human!

I focused with all my power on that one thought. I squeezed my eyes shut and tried to remember who I was. What I looked like.

I felt my body change. It was a horrifying sensation. I could hear bones crunching. I could feel a sudden nausea as a human stomach reappeared. I seemed to itch all over as flesh absorbed feathers.

Had I done this before? It didn't seem possible. It was disgusting. Grotesque.

I opened my eyes.

Right above me! What was it?

Mouths with needle-sharp teeth! Staring eyes! Whirling blades!

It was after me!

Should I fly? Should I run? What was I?

I leapt up, hoping I had legs.

Yes! I could run. Yes! I ran. I ran! My own bare feet flashed ahead of me. Human feet. My arms pumped, but they still felt odd. The bones were connected wrong. I ran! Over pine needles that stabbed the tender soles of my feet.

B-R-R-A-A-A-K-K!

It was behind me! It chewed through a tree four feet thick. Chewed it up and left splinters and sawdust behind.

"NO!" I screamed, and my voice was almost human.

NO! NO! It was after me. It wanted to kill me. Why? Why? What had I done? Who was I, that this monster wanted to destroy me?

I raced as fast as I could, but it was faster. Entire trees were ripped from the ground to make way for it. The very ground itself was ripped up as if by some huge plow. The shrieking of destruction was all around me.

What was happening to me?

"Help me!" I screamed. And now my voice was truly human. The last of the changes were occurring. My arms pumped smoothly now. My eyes looked past a normal human nose. The beak was gone.

But the beast . . . the BEAST! It was on me!

Suddenly, a road! Cars flashing by!

I ran for the road. The beast pursued me, ripping a path through the woods.

Cars zooming past! If I ran out into the road, they would hit me. If I stopped, the beast would devour me.

I ran.

SWOOOOM! A car shot past, missing me by inches. Six lanes! A freeway! I ran, hoping against hope to survive.

Horns! Blaring horns!

A truck.

The beast.

It hit the truck, or the truck hit it. I don't know which.

The cabin of the truck was crumpled. I caught a flash of the driver yelling, frantically working the steering wheel.

Then the trailer part, the part that said BEN AND JERRY'S, slammed into the dust beast.

Screeching, screaming wheels! Then, WHAM!

I tripped and went sprawling into the median strip. I rolled down a grassy slope into dirty water. I looked up in time to see the truck turn over and skid wildly down the freeway, spraying sparks.

The beast shredded the trailer. Shredded it! Pints of ice cream exploded around like hand grenades. In the middle of terror I was pelted by pints of Cherry Garcia and Wavy Gravy ice cream.

The beast rose from the truck. The driver climbed up out of the cab and ran.

As the beast rose into the air, a hundred manic eyes looked around. It saw me. There was no doubt about that, it SAW me.

But the eyes seemed confused. They seemed lost. The beast saw me, but did not recognize me.

Suddenly, as I cowered in the ditch of the median strip, the beast simply dissolved into a cloud of dust.

Dissolved and blew away.

Traffic had stopped on all six lanes, as people hung out their windows to witness the spectacle of a tractor-trailer lying across the road.

I climbed shakily out of the ditch. I was trembling so badly I could barely stand. I was muddy and wet and barefoot, wearing a black leotard. I stumbled across the road, toward the sheltering woods.

A man with a camcorder emerged from his car and began taping the wreck. From far off came the wail of a siren.

I just wanted to get away.

Whoever I was.

PREUSS SCHOOL

CHAPTER 9
Cassie

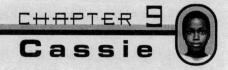

"Tornado my butt," Marco said angrily. "That thing was alive."

We were watching TV in my living room. Jake, Marco, Ax in his human morph, and me, Cassie. It was afternoon. My parents weren't home yet, so we were safe, talking freely.

The news was doing a special report. They had broken into a talk show to show film of what they described as a "freak tornado." They were showing what was left of Darlene's house. The reporter was standing right where we'd had the pool party. You could see Darlene in the background with her parents, picking through the wreckage.

"The storm hit late this morning, just before

noon," the reporter said. "Some young people were having a pool party, and they describe a sort of funnel cloud that appeared quite suddenly out of a clear sky. Some of the kids who were here actually described it as seeming like a monster or a beast. But of course they were quite frightened at the time."

"They were frightened, all right," Marco muttered. "They were wetting their pants. I know."

"The house was virtually destroyed," the reporter went on. "Almost miraculously, there were only some minor injuries. A few of the kids suffered abrasions and minor cuts. The house itself was fully insured."

"That's a good thing," Marco said dryly. "Because we're talking a lot more than a paint job needed there."

"Now let's go out to the freeway where the same tornado — or possibly a second tornado — destroyed a tractor-trailer, holding up traffic for hours."

The screen showed a Ben and Jerry's ice-cream truck that looked like it had been blown apart by a bomb.

Suddenly I saw something familiar.

"Hey! Look!" I said.

"What?" Jake asked.

"It's gone now," I said. "Are we taping this?"

"Yeah," Marco said. "What is it?"

"Back the tape up. Back it up."

Marco reversed the VCR tape. I watched as the camera panned back across the wreck. Then . . .

"Right there! Right there!" I said. "That girl. See? She's only in the shot for a second. Can you freeze-frame her?"

"Why?" Jake asked. "What is it?"

Marco rewound, then advanced the tape a frame at a time. A blurry figure appeared. The frame froze.

"What is the matter?" Ax asked. "Matt-ter? Ter."

Ax can be odd when he's in human morph. Having a mouth and being able to make sounds just fascinates him.

"Look at that girl," I said. "Tall. Blond hair. Barefoot. Wearing a black leotard."

Jake's eyes widened in shocked recognition. So did Marco's.

"Oh, my God," Marco whispered. "It is! It's Rachel. It has to be."

"She must have just come out of a morph," I said. "That's her morphing suit. And being barefoot and all?"

See, when we morph we can't morph much clothing — just something skintight. And shoes? Forget shoes. I've tried morphing shoes. They end up looking like an entire pack of dogs played tug-of-war with them.

"What is Rachel doing out there?" Jake demanded. "She's supposed to be up in the mountains at that camp."

"You know what this means?" Marco demanded. "That thing. That *thing* that came after Ax and me was also right where Rachel was. Coincidence? I don't think so."

Jake shook his head. "No. Not a coincidence." He looked at Ax. "Do you know what this is?"

"No," Ax said. "I do not. It is not any race that I have ever heard of. But I agree: It is no coincidence. Cidence. Co-IN-sid-DENSE."

"Well, what is it?" Marco demanded angrily.

"Tobias told us that it headed toward the forest at a very high speed," I said. "It was heading for Rachel. The timing is right. The location is right. It attacked Marco and Ax, but then it stopped and went tearing off for Rachel."

"Why? What is the point? If it's some Yeerk weapon, it should have finished us off. I mean, it had Ax and me cold."

"We need to talk to Rachel," Jake said. "Cassie?"

"I'll call." I went to the phone, the one in the kitchen. I dialed Rachel's number. I've probably dialed that number every day for years.

On the third ring: "Hello?"

"Hi, Jordan." Jordan is Rachel's younger sister. "Is Rachel home?"

"Duh, Cassie. She's at the gymnastics thing. The camp."

I felt a tingling up my spine. "So . . . so she did go?"

"Sure."

"She didn't come back early or anything?"

"No. Why? Is something the matter?"

"Nah. Nothing. I was just thinking maybe . . . never mind. Later."

I hung up the phone and took several deep breaths. I didn't want to alarm the others. I went back to the living room.

Marco was still yelling at the guy on the TV. "It wasn't a tornado! Are people blind? A tornado does not have teeth."

Jake saw me first. I tried to conceal the fear I felt inside. But I can't hide anything from Jake. He knows me too well.

"What is it?" he asked.

"Rachel. She isn't home. They think she's at the camp."

Jake, Marco, and Ax all just stared for a moment. Then Marco rewound the tape and played it back.

Tall, blond, a model's body, wearing a black leotard and no shoes.

It was Rachel.

And she was definitely not at camp.

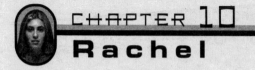

CHAPTER 10
Rachel

I spent hours just walking in the woods. Walking and trying to remember.

Who was I?

What was I?

I didn't know. My mind would not answer me.

I remembered how to talk. I remembered what things were called. I knew that the sky was blue, and the moon was white, and the ocean was deep, and that winter was colder than summer.

I knew all the background things of life. It was like watching a TV show where you could see all the sets, but the characters were invisible.

Of me — of who I was and what I was — I knew nothing.

Or not quite nothing. I knew that I was some sort of freak. I knew I could have the feathers and beak and legs of a bird.

And I knew that I had some terrible enemy.

The pine needles and fallen branches made walking painful. But what else could I do? Where was I supposed to go? Some terrible beast was hunting me. Who could I possibly trust?

"Answer me!" I yelled at no one but the trees. "Who am I?"

The sound of my own voice reminded me I had to be careful. The beast from the sky might be out there. Might still be looking for me.

I walked, always hoping the clouds would lift from my memory. I knew I had amnesia. I remembered the word "amnesia." But how had it happened? *That* I could not remember.

I stayed fairly close to the highway that sliced through the forest. I could see flashes of cars through the trees, a few hundred yards off to my right. But I stayed deep enough in the woods that no one from the road could see me.

I could not afford to be seen. Not until I knew what danger I was in.

Then, amidst all the greens and browns of the forest, I saw something bright yellow. It was deeper in the woods. Another few hundred yards deeper.

I crouched down low and walked on bent legs

toward the splash of yellow. I moved as quietly as I could, placing each bare foot carefully.

It was a shack. The yellow was a cotton, ribbed top. From The Limited, probably.

I froze. What? From The Limited? What did that mean? I squeezed my eyes shut and concentrated.

FLASH! A store. It was a store. Clothing. Tables covered with folded tops in bright colors. I was there. I was there shopping with . . . I knew there was someone with me. I could *feel* the fact that someone was with me.

But I couldn't see any more. The memory fragment was only a brief snippet of time. It told me nothing.

I looked again at the shack. It looked like it had been built a long time ago. It was made of logs, some of which were rotted out. Had I been here before? It felt familiar. This place . . . a place like it . . . but no. I was probably just imagining things.

The yellow top was hanging on a clothesline. I duckwalked left to see through the front doorway. It was open. There was no light inside the cabin.

Should I? Could I take the risk?

"If you want to return the item you'll need a receipt," a voice said.

"Yaaahhh!" I yelled, and spun around.

A woman. Old. No, not so old. Just shabby. Wearing so many layers of clothing she looked fat. But she wasn't. She was thin. Dragging a bulging canvas bag.

Not a threat.

I forced myself to calm down. I tried to let the adrenaline flow out of me, but my heart was pounding and my muscles were tensed.

"You'll need a receipt," the woman said again. She stared at me in a challenging way and held out her hand.

"What?" I asked. "Do you know me?"

"If you want to return the item you'll need a receipt," she said again. She said it precisely the way she had the first time. The identical inflection.

She was insane.

"I don't have a receipt," I said.

She looked past me at something. Or nothing. Then she headed for the shack. I don't know why, but I followed her.

She was mentally ill, but she didn't seem dangerous. And I wasn't exactly normal myself.

I don't know what I expected to find inside the shack, but it was a shock: clothing. Piles of it three feet high. In every corner, clothing. Much of it was dirty. Filthy. Some was stained or burned. Some seemed fine.

The madwoman ignored me completely. She

opened her dirty canvas bag and began pulling out more items of clothing. Stained shirts. Ripped jeans. One old sneaker.

"Excuse me," I said. "Ma'am?"

"If you want to return the item you'll need a receipt."

"Can you tell me your name?"

She stopped sorting the clothing. She turned a sly grin toward me. "*My* name? Or *its* name? We are two, not one. Yes. Yes. If you want to return the item —"

"*Your* name, please," I said.

"It's gone now," she said craftily. "But it will be back. Oh yes, they'll be back. They never go away forever."

I guess normally I might have been frustrated. I might have even gotten annoyed. But I knew now what it was like to have your brain betray you.

"Who does all this clothing belong to?" I asked.

"MINE!" she shrieked suddenly. "MINE! It's MINE!"

"Okay, okay! Okay. It's yours."

"I found it all. People throw it away. It's mine."

"Yes, it's yours. But I was wondering . . . I don't have any shoes. I thought maybe you could let me borrow a pair of shoes."

"Will that be cash, check, or credit card?"

"I . . . um . . ." I had an idea. Maybe it was

stupid. Maybe it was even a little cruel. I bent down and picked up a chunk of pine bark from the floor. I held it out to the woman. "Credit card."

She took it. She looked at it in confusion. Then she looked up at me. There was something lost and desperate in her eyes. "Is this the store?" she asked.

"It's your store," I said.

She forced a shaky smile. "Let me know if I can help you find anything."

"I will," I said.

I began digging through the nearest pile of clothing. Shoes were stuck here and there. I dug each one out, one by one, and set them in a pile on the floor. I needed a size five. So far I had mostly men's shoes.

"Are you one of *them*?" the woman asked.

"One of what, ma'am?" I replied.

"The others. The ones who live in your head."

"I don't think so," I said. I was focused on my search.

"There's only one way to know for sure," she said in a soft, silky voice.

Success! One size six Reebok, and one size five Converse. They weren't exactly matched, but they were better than being barefoot.

I heard a creak of rusty hinges behind me. I turned to look. The old woman had opened a trapdoor in the floor of the shack.

I started to rise from my crouch, holding the shoes.

WHUMPF!

Something hit me from behind. I tried to suck in a breath, but the blow had emptied my lungs. The woman was all over me, shoving, clawing, scratching, and screaming.

"YEERK! YEERK! YEERK!"

I struggled to fend her off, but she was strong and driven by her insane vision.

I fell. Down through the hole in the floor.

"YEERK! YEERK!" she screamed.

I landed on dirt. I recovered quickly and leaped back up at the opening. The hatch slammed down on me.

I ducked, just in time.

"YEERK! YEERK! YEERK!"

FLASH! A gray, sludgy pool. An underground cavern. Something in the pool, swimming. Many somethings. Seething just beneath the surface of the pool. Like fish. No . . . slugs. Gray slugs.

"YEERK!"

My head swam with the sudden vision. But I couldn't focus on that. I had to get out. I pounded on the splintery wood of the hatch. "Lady, let me out of here! Let me out of here! I don't want to hurt you."

No answer. I looked around. It wasn't a basement. Just a space beneath the shack. Maybe long, long ago it had been some kind of way to escape. Or maybe it was a place to store food for the winter. But it had the feeling of great age.

It was hard-packed dirt on three sides. The fourth side was a wall of vertical logs. I could see through the gaps in the logs. But I did not see a way out.

"Lady, let me out of here. I'm not going to hurt you."

She spoke in a much quieter voice. "No, no. You don't want to hurt me. You just want to crawl inside my head. Like you did before. Crawl inside my head . . . make me . . . make me give you my husband. Make me give him to you. My children. All for you. All for YOU. Controlling me. In my head. But you died, didn't you, Yeerk?"

I felt a terrible coldness. She was insane. *Insane.* And yet . . . why did her raving mean something to me? That word . . . *Yeerk*. It meant something. Something evil.

Was I crazy, too? Was that the truth I was hiding from myself?

CHAPTER 11
Jake

Marco and I took the bus to a place close to where the dust beast had attacked Rachel and destroyed the ice-cream truck.

The bus stopped and we climbed off. We were at a combination gas station and convenience store just off the highway. There was a Denny's across the street and a Dairy Queen not far off.

The wreckage of the Ben and Jerry's truck was at the gas station. It had been towed there to get it off the road. There wasn't much left of the trailer. It had been chewed up and ground into splinters.

"Well," Marco said dryly, "that sure looks like the work of the same creature that ventilated Darlene's house."

"You do realize you shouldn't have been there in the first place," I said. "Someone could have been killed."

"Like I knew some devil beast was going to come after me?" Marco demanded.

I let it go. Marco knew he'd screwed up. At least, I hoped he knew.

"Come on," I said. "You have the bag?"

"Of course I have the bag," Marco grumbled.

We headed for the woods. Once well into the trees we began scanning the tree branches.

<Up here,> Tobias said in thought-speak.

He was on a branch, preening his feathers. He used his beak to sort of comb through each feather.

"Is this really the time to be worrying about your looks?" Marco asked.

<Preening isn't about looks,> Tobias said patiently. <I'm cleaning and straightening feathers. Clean feathers fly better.>

"How do you even get dirty?" Marco wondered. "I mean, flying all the time . . ."

<I was hungry, so I ate a mouse. A mouse just like the one you became this morning,> Tobias said. <It wasn't a very clean kill. Any other questions?>

I smiled as Marco turned slightly green.

"Where's Ax?" I asked.

<He's coming. He's about a mile back. He's fast, but he's on foot, whereas I flew.>

"Did you . . ."

<No,> Tobias answered. <I didn't see anything. No humans walking in this area of the woods at all, as far as I saw. Except for this crazy woman who lives in a shack out here. No Rachel.>

"Okay," I said, "Marco and I are going to morph now. You want to go up top and make sure we're clear?"

Tobias opened his wings and swept low over our heads before catching a headwind and rising up above the treetops.

"Ready, Marco?" I asked.

"Sure. I love this morph. It's cool. This is what morphing should always be like."

We were planning to use our wolf morphs. For one thing, wolves ran in the forest, so we wouldn't be totally out of place. But more importantly, wolves have a magnificent sense of smell.

"Open the bag."

Marco opened the bag and took out a girl's shirt. It belonged to Rachel. She'd left it at Cassie's house. We hoped it would still smell like Rachel. We were going to play bloodhound. We shoved our clothes back into the bag and stood there in our morphing suits — bike shorts and tops. Needless to say, we looked just a bit out of place.

<All clear,> Tobias called down from somewhere above.

"Well, let's do it," I said to Marco.

"You look so Ah-nold when you get that expression," Marco teased.

"So what?"

"So Arnold. Schwarzenegger."

I smiled. "Oh, shut up."

"All ride den, led's do id," Marco said, doing a pretty decent Arnold accent.

I focused on the wolf. We had first acquired the wolf morphs a while back, when we were on a mission to destroy a Yeerk truck ship.

Wolf, I said to myself.

The first change was the fur, gray and shaggy and as rough as carpeting. It sprouted from my human skin in a wave that rippled down from my neck all across my body.

I could see my face bulging out, growing a long snout. It's very odd, because when you're a human you can't really see your own nose. So it's definitely weird to have this long thing sticking out of your face.

Of course, that's not exactly the only weird thing about morphing.

Morphing seems like it should hurt. I mean, there are entire organs inside your body that are changing. Even down to individual cells, everything about you is changed within a couple of minutes.

It doesn't hurt, though. I guess the Andalite scientists who discovered the process made sure of that. If it had hurt, it would have been pain too terrible to live through. Especially when you're doing some really bizarre morph, like into a lobster or an ant, when there's almost nothing left that's even slightly human.

It didn't hurt. But it could definitely creep you out. I could hear my bones shifting and popping and stretching and squeezing. There was a grinding noise when my knee suddenly reversed direction.

"Hey, Jake?" Marco said. He still had most of his human mouth.

I started to answer him. But the sound that came out was more like "Yowwrrllrow."

Marco grinned and at that second his mouth bulged into a snout. His teeth grew and multiplied and became the fearsome weapons of the wolf.

<I don't believe it. It's coming!> Tobias yelled. <It's coming!>

I didn't need to ask what Tobias meant. I looked up at the sky. A dust storm was blowing just above the trees.

<It's coming!>

CHAPTER 12

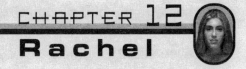

Rachel

"Let me out, you crazy old woman!" I yelled.

I was learning something about myself. I still didn't know my own name, but I knew one thing: Whoever I was, I had a temper.

But the woman was no longer paying attention to me. I could hear her in the cabin above, sorting clothes and muttering to herself.

The anger I felt was good. I realized it kept me from being afraid. There was something about that word . . . "Yeerk" . . . It meant something. Something bad.

FLASH! I was looking through strange eyes. Seeing too well. Seeing not at all. Then . . . a centipede! Bigger than a human, huge! More creatures. Some real, some . . . some that couldn't possibly be real. An elephant . . . a massive, rampaging bear . . . ants that were as big as I was . . . a deadly creature that swung razor-bladed arms and had feet like tyrannosaurs and . . .

FLASH! . . . and a creature dying. Like a horse. No, like a deer. But not a deer. A tail that flashed. Eyes . . . too many eyes. And thoughts! Thoughts that were in my head.

"Get out of my head!" I yelled suddenly.

I gasped. It had been so powerful. My mind had opened and gushed out horrible images. Then it had closed again. Everything was hidden once more beneath a gray blanket.

I smelled smoke.

And the scent was strong. Strong and near. Was the old woman cooking? Making a campfire. Was she . . .

The shack! It was burning!

"Let me out of here!" I cried. "The shack's on fire!"

"You won't get me again, Yeerk!"

"I'm not a Yeerk! Let me out! Let me out!"

The fire spread with stunning swiftness. In less than a minute there were tongues of flame dripping down through the chinks in the floor above me. I could hear it snapping and popping. The smoke poured down in gusts and then blew away, only to come back still stronger.

"Let me out!" I yelled again. But there was no answer.

I was going to burn! I coughed as smoke scorched my throat. I ran to the log uprights that formed the cage. I shoved at them — shoved and pulled, but they didn't move.

I was trapped!

I tried to scream again, but I coughed instead. I could barely breathe. Already my head was feeling light.

Power. I needed power to break out. Power enough to shatter the rotted logs!

I sank to my knees, driven down by the heat. Sparks fell around me, and I brushed them away as they burned my legs and back.

I was too weak. I couldn't do it. But within me . . . something within me . . .

And then it began. I didn't even notice it at first. I was too terrified. I expected the flame-engulfed cabin to crash down on me at any moment.

Suddenly, I began to change.

I was becoming large. So large, so quickly, that my head was rising toward the flames.

Heavy, dark brown fur was growing from my arms and legs.

But what I noticed most was the power. Rippling, massive muscles bulged from my arms and legs and swelled my neck. It was an incredible, giddy rush.

One minute, I was weak and failing and nearing death. The next minute . . . the power! The amazing, straining, bulging, explosive POWER!

CHAPTER 13

Marco

Tobias came shooting down toward us. He wanted to make sure we knew.

<It's coming!>

I was halfway into morph. Could I use thought-speak yet? I decided to try. <We hear you, Tobias. I can see it.>

<Finish morphing,> Jake yelled in my head. <Better to face this thing as wolves.>

I was trembling with fear. I had faced this thing once already that day. I wasn't interested in facing it twice. But Jake was right — better to fight as a wolf than as a human. And this time Jake was with me.

I was on all fours. I could feel the wolf's strength. I could sense the intelligence and instincts of the wolf's brain. All the wolf's incredible senses were mine.

But when I looked up to see the beast forming, I knew the wolf wasn't nearly enough. No animal morph could fight this thing!

<Look at it!> I cried.

<Yeah,> Jake said. He was trying to sound brave. But Jake's been my friend for many years. I know when he's scared. He was scared plenty.

<Here it comes!>

The beast of a hundred mouths and a hundred whirling blades came for us. There were treetops in the way. The beast shredded them.

B-R-R-R-A-A-A-A-K!

We ran. It would have been stupid to do anything else. My powerful wolf's jaws were nothing to this beast.

I ran, and I ran fast. Wolves have pretty good speed, and incredible endurance. A wolf can run for hours, all day if necessary. But I didn't think I would get the chance to run that long.

The beast dropped to just a few feet above the ground, leveled off, and came after us. The trees were close together. Too tight for the beast to fit through, so it simply shredded anything in its way.

B-R-R-R-A-A-A-A-K!

The noise was shocking. I ran. I leapt over fallen logs. I dodged around trees. I counted on my rough gray coat to protect me as I ripped straight through thorn bushes.

B-R-R-R-A-A-A-A-K!

The beast ripped a path fifty feet wide through the forest. It was like some nightmare lumberjack. It reduced trees to twigs and splinters in seconds. Wood shrapnel flew everywhere.

<It's gaining!> I said to Jake. <Little by little, it's gaining!>

<The trees. It destroys them, but they slow it down. Just enough.>

<More trees. Thicker trees!> I yelled.

I looked wildly around at a world washed pale by the wolf's poor color vision. There were trees everywhere. Too many! I didn't know which way the forest grew denser and which way it might thin out.

But the wolf knew. The wolf's own instincts led the way. Jake and I both felt it, I guess, because we began turning north.

B-R-R-R-A-A-A-A-K!

The trees grew thicker and there were more of them. The beast chewed its way after us, but it was no longer gaining.

It was not falling behind, either.

<Jake! Marco! What are you doing?> Tobias yelled.

<Heading for denser woods,> Jake said. <Maybe it'll slow this thing down!>

<It is getting thicker up ahead,> Tobias agreed. <But you better hope it wears out soon.>

<Why?> I said.

<Because you have a quarter mile of woods. And then it opens up into a meadow,> Tobias said. <Open grass.>

Jake and I said nothing. We didn't have to. We both knew if the beast didn't tire out before we came out into open country, it would catch us.

And it didn't seem tired.

Just then, as terrified as I was, I smelled something that set off deeper alarm bells in the wolf's mind. Smoke. There was a fire not far away.

And to my acute wolf's ears came the faintest sound of a human voice screaming.

Just as if the beast had heard the same faint cry, I saw the monster shudder. It hesitated.

<Jake! Look!>

The beast wavered and slowed. I could see the meadow through the trees. The meadow where we would surely die.

Except that now the beast was wavering. Suddenly, it turned away.

It turned toward the place that smelled of fire and smoke.

CHAPTER 14

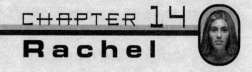

Rachel

"Aaaaarrrrgghh!" I cried.

I was in a shower of flames, as bits of wood and fabric fell around me. I couldn't breathe. I couldn't see. But I could hear an insane grinding noise from deep within my own body. And I knew that I was changing.

In all my despair, I could feel the power flowing through me. Awesome power. But was it enough?

I waited as long as I could. I wasn't done changing. But the heat was too great. And the thing that I was becoming hated the fire.

A sudden surge of muscles! A forward rush! I slammed into the half-rotted logs.

Crrr-RUNCH!

The logs broke from the force of my huge body. The logs that had imprisoned me were mere sticks now. I hurtled through them and away from the burning shack.

At that moment, the shack collapsed on itself in an explosion of sparks.

I stood panting. I stood on four legs. I looked down and saw front paws where hands should have been. My paws were covered in coarse brown fur, very shaggy. And I had long, sharp black claws.

FLASH! A bear on its hind legs, roaring and swinging its mighty paws. Creatures all around. Like walking razor blades. They came for the bear . . . came for *me*.

Yes! I thought. *Grizzly bear*. That was it. I had become a bear. Was still *becoming* a bear, because the morphing was not completely done.

"What am I?" I shouted. But the sound that came from my mouth was not human. "Hhhhhu-uuuRORW!"

What kind of creature was I? How could I do this? How could I become a different animal? It was insane. Insane.

Maybe it was that simple. Maybe I was as insane as the woman who had burned down her shack to kill me for being a Yeerk.

Was that it? Was I a Yeerk? What was a Yeerk?

Suddenly, I heard a wild rush of wind. Not

from the burning, crumbling cabin — from above. Up in the air. I looked up, but my human eyes were changing to bear eyes and I couldn't see very well. I only saw a large shadow hovering above me.

A flash of swift movement! It was attacking!

The last of my human body was gone. And now I felt the full force of the grizzly bear's own mind. It was unafraid. And more than that, it was angry.

No one attacked a grizzly. Not if they wanted to live.

I reared up on my hind legs. I must have been ten feet tall. And I knew I was mighty.

"HhhhuuRRRROOOOWWWWRRRR!" I roared. I swung my massive paw at the hovering beast.

But then, a second flash of movement. Another animal, racing swiftly toward us.

<Rachel! Rachel, is that you?> a voice demanded. A voice I did not truly hear, except inside my head.

I looked at the new creature. It had come to a stop, just a dozen feet away. I peered at it with my dim bear vision. It had four legs, like a horse or a deer. But it seemed to have a head and upper body that was almost human. And there was a tail, I was sure of that. The tail was cocked back like a weapon ready to be fired.

For a frozen moment of time, we all three

waited: me, the beast in the air, and this new apparition.

<Rachel. Rachel. Is that you in morph? It's me, Ax.>

<Rachel?> I asked silently. <Is that my name?>

And then the beast made of dust attacked.

CHAPTER 15

Ax

My name is Aximili-Esgarrouth-Isthill. I am an Andalite. It was my brother, Prince Elfangor, who gave the humans the power to morph. He had been injured trying to drive the Yeerks away from Earth. And, when he crash-landed his fighter, it was Jake, Rachel, Tobias, Cassie, and Marco who found him.

It was Visser Three who killed my brother, so my human friends have told me. Someday I will avenge that death. I must kill Visser Three or be dishonored.

Later, Jake and the others found me. I was the last surviving Andalite from our great Dome ship.

I am not one of the Animorphs. But I fight

alongside them against our common enemy, the Yeerks. And while I am on Earth, I have taken Jake for my prince.

I had gone along with Marco on his foolish venture to the home of the human named Darlene. I knew it was foolish, but I thought it would be better for Marco to have someone with him.

Marco is highly intelligent. But he is also very afflicted by a condition the humans call "sense of humor." I have noticed that Marco's sense of humor sometimes makes him do strange things.

But when the great beast from the sky appeared, I was powerless. Later, the humans asked me for answers. Did I know what this beast was? The humans assume that I must know every terrible thing that lives in this vast galaxy.

But I did not know this creature. And it frightened me.

When we set off to find Rachel, I traveled through the woods. I live in the forest now. It is my new home.

I ran steadily to reach the place where I was to meet up with Tobias, Jake, and Marco.

Then I detected the smoke. I looked up and saw a pillar of smoke rising through the trees.

My eyes swept around me, checking every direction. I must always be very careful not to be seen by humans. One stalk eye followed the pillar of smoke into the sky. And then, I saw not smoke, but dust. Dust that blew faster than any wind.

The beast!

It was coming again.

I ran! Faster than before, with all my speed.

It had to be looking for me. It had come to hunt me down, I was sure of it. Where should I run? Not toward where Jake and Marco were supposed to be. I could not lead the beast to them.

But the fire . . . maybe the smoke would hide me. Yes!

I raced toward the smell of smoke. My hooves flashed, my tail was tucked down tight against my back for speed.

I saw a small clearing. And in the clearing, a pillar of flame. A building of some sort. It was burning rapidly. The heat blasted me. I could hear the noise of dry wood snapping and popping, flames sucking at the air.

But there was a greater noise. The beast! Above me, above the fire, it swirled and roared like a storm.

Then I saw another creature. It was an Earth animal called a grizzly bear. It reared up on its hind legs and bellowed defiance. But that mighty voice was swallowed up in the hurricane howl of the dust beast.

A grizzly bear. Rachel had a grizzly bear morph. I had seen her use it. It had to be her.

<Rachel! Rachel, is that you?>

The huge bear swung its massive head to glare at me. But there was no thought-speak answer.

<Rachel. Rachel. Is that you in morph? It's me, Ax.>

<Rachel? Is that my name?>

Suddenly, the dust beast attacked.

In a rush of hurricane winds, it descended on Rachel. Not on me, but on Rachel! It was her the beast wanted.

She stood firm, unafraid.

<Rachel!> I cried. <Run, you can't fight it!>

The beast of a hundred gnashing mouths descended on the bear. The bear swung a massive paw. It was a blow that would have knocked my head from my shoulders. A blow that would have punched through steel.

The claws raked the dust beast's closest mouth.

"ROOOWWWWRRR!" the bear cried in sudden pain.

Its paw was gone! Simply *gone*. In its place was a shattered, bloody stump.

What could I do? I was desperate. My tail was my only weapon. But the creature would simply grind it off as he'd done with Rachel's paw.

Rachel bellowed in pain from her awful wound, but she struck again. Still standing erect and defiant, she struck again with her other paw.

"HhhhRRROOOOAAAARR!"

This time the entire leg was gone! And now I could see human terror shining through the bear's eyes.

<Rachel!> I cried in despair.

My Andalite tail was useless. I needed something else. Anything! I searched my memory. What morph did I have to fight this monster?

Nothing. Nothing. Rachel's bear was one of the mightiest morphs we had. And she was doomed.

There was nothing left now but to escape.

No! Not to escape. To follow this creature. To find where it hid. To find where it came from.

I had an Earth bird morph. It was called a harrier. It was very fast. I could morph and perhaps be able to follow this monster.

Because one thing was certain: I could not save Rachel.

The dust beast descended on Rachel. It enveloped her completely. I could no longer see her. It was as if a cloud was swallowing her up. The beast shifted and flowed and re-formed to engulf the raging bear that was my human friend, Rachel.

Shaking with fury and horror, I began to morph.

And suddenly, with a speed that was shocking, the dust beast stopped.

It lifted away from Rachel.

It exploded upward, away from her, and came at me! Right at me!

And in the few seconds left to me, I realized . . . *the morphing!* It was the morphing! That's what it was after. It was reacting to the morphing. It was the morphing energy itself that drew the beast.

It lifted from Rachel. I had a flash of her bear body, wrapped in living ropes. The beast had not killed her. It had wrapped her up, as if wrapping a gift.

The living ropes dissolved to rejoin the dust beast and become part of it.

A hundred mouths and a thousand whirling blades descended on me. Now it was after me! And I knew that if I struck it with my tail, it would leave me with a bloody stump.

I could not fight it. To fight was to be shredded.

I stood still. I reversed the morph and regained my complete Andalite form.

I felt the beast around me. It suffocated me. It choked me. It wrapped me tightly in a cocoon till I could not move an inch.

I felt myself being lifted up from the ground. Up and up, faster and faster, unable to see, able only to hear the wild winds of the beast itself.

But now I understood. I knew where it was taking me.

I knew the purpose of the beast.

And with a fear that chilled me to my bones, I realized that I knew its master's name.

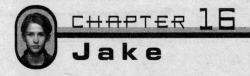

CHAPTER 16

Jake

My wolf nose told me a story.

The stench of burning wood was everywhere, but I could still smell blood. Something had sprayed blood over a wide area. A bear. I smelled the powerful scent of a bear.

I sniffed the ground again. Human. Two different humans.

And something else . . . a strange, alien smell. A smell like nothing I could imagine. Until I looked at the tracks: sharp hoof marks. Ax. Ax had been here.

Two humans. One wearing shoes. One barefoot. A bear. Ax. Blood. A fire, still smoldering.

<What do you make of it?> I asked Marco.

<The barefoot person had to be Rachel. So

was the bear. It had to be her. There are no grizzlies in this forest. And the blood, that's hers, too. Or the bear's, anyway. So she was hurt bad.>

I swallowed anger and fear. I had to stay focused. <What can hurt a grizzly?> I asked, knowing the answer.

<A man with a gun,> Marco said. <Another grizzly. Or some animal that isn't from Earth. No Earth animal can mess with a grizzly bear.>

<It was that *thing*,> I said.

Tobias swooped down low and slow. <Bear tracks head north. I see tracks, but they're weird. Hind legs only. Like the bear was walking erect. And blood.>

<So Rachel in bear morph tangled with the dust beast,> I said. <She came out of it alive, but she couldn't use her front paws.>

<That's the way it looks,> Tobias said. <The bear tracks stop down by a stream maybe a thousand yards from here. After that, I don't see anything. She must have morphed back to human.>

<Which way did she go?> Marco asked. <Upstream? Downstream?>

Tobias came to rest on a branch. <I don't know. I looked. I didn't see her. I should have gotten here sooner. I should have known when it let you two go that it was going off after her.>

<Tobias, no one understands this monster. You couldn't have known what it would do. None

of us could,> I said. It sounded reasonable. But in my mind I was thinking that I should have known. I should have guessed.

<What's Ax's story in all this?> I asked. Blaming myself was not the point right now. <Ax was coming to meet us. He sees the fire, goes to investigate it. Maybe then he sees Rachel? Or Rachel in bear morph? Were they both here at the same time?>

<I don't know,> Marco said. <Maybe. Lots of Andalite tracks all together here. Then, look — they just stop. Right here. No Andalite scent past this point. It's like he was just lifted up and carried away.>

Tobias said, <So he gets here, sees Rachel and the beast going at it. Ax is a brave guy. He jumps into it. Rachel gets away. She's bloody, but she gets away. And Ax? Why isn't he still here? Or else why don't we see a separate set of Andalite tracks leaving? Or at least see his body?>

No one said anything. We all feared the worst. I was remembering what the beast had done to Darlene's house. And to the trees. Maybe it didn't leave bodies behind. Maybe there was no body left after it was done.

<Andalites are tougher than they look,> Tobias said. <I'm with Ax a lot, out here in the forest. Don't write him off.>

<Yeah,> I agreed, trying to sound hopeful. <We've been in morph a long time. We need to use what time we have left to get to civilization and morph back. I have to at least check in with my folks or they'll have cops out looking for me.>

<We can't just stop looking,> Marco said. <Tobias only has an hour of good light left. After that, there won't be anyone trying to find Rachel. Or Ax.>

<I'll use that hour,> Tobias said. He opened his wings and flapped wearily back up into the sky.

<We'll come back tonight,> I told Marco. <Have dinner with your dad. Then we hook up at Cassie's barn.>

<Jake, what is going on?> Marco asked me as we trotted swiftly back toward the road. <Is this the Yeerks?>

<Who else could it be?> I asked.

<But look, if it's them, then they know who we are. I mean, this thing came right after me and Ax. It went after Rachel. It went after me and you. It *knows* who we are. So why don't the Yeerks just move in on us? Why not show up at our homes?>

<That's the question,> I agreed. We had reached the road. The bus would come by soon. It was time to demorph. <That is exactly the question we need to answer.>

<Yeah, that and the question of where Rachel is, and why she doesn't go home.>

<And one more question,> I added, as I felt my human body emerge from within the wolf. <How do we stay alive?>

CHAPTER 17

Cassie

Radio Shack. August Woman. Godiva. The Gap. Mrs. Field's. Casual Corner. B. Dalton. Kinney Shoes. Banana Republic.

Bright lights. Color. Signs. The smell of cinnamon buns.

The mall. Yuck.

And worse yet, the mall on a Saturday evening. It was crowded. It was loud. But the mall was the place to look for Rachel.

Jake, Marco, Tobias, and Ax had all gone to the spot where the ice-cream truck attack had taken place. Jake had asked me to look in all the other places she might have gone. He'd said I would know best where she hung out.

Maybe that was true, but it bothered me a little. It could be a little sexist on Jake's part. Or maybe he was trying to protect me. Either way, it bothered me. I didn't want special treatment because I was a girl. Jake would never even think about something like that with Rachel.

It bothered me for another reason, too. It bothered me because a part of me was just a little relieved. I was safe in the mall. Who knew what Jake and the others were dealing with out in the forest?

I told myself I wasn't glad to be safe. I told myself I was just doing what needed to be done. But the possibility that Jake was in danger, while I was safe, gnawed away at me.

It's because you told Jake about the stupid dream, I realized. *Now he thinks you're losing it. Not a surprise, is it? Tell a guy you're having nightmares where you face evil and choose who it kills, he's going to maybe think you're losing it.*

Just the same, Jake was right: I knew the places Rachel might go.

I had already checked out the gym where Rachel did gymnastics, and the frozen yogurt place where she always ordered key lime pie flavor. I'd checked school, just because that's where she should have caught the bus. And I had scoped out her house, even though her sister said she wasn't there.

Which left the mall.

"Wait. Is that her?" I muttered to myself. I stood on tiptoes to see better. No. It was some other blond girl.

I am not a shopper. To me, shopping is something you do when you have to. For Rachel, it is an art form. If she wasn't at home, she should be here.

"Rachel?" I called loudly to a girl passing by. But as soon as I did, I knew it wasn't her. "Sorry. Thought I knew you."

Then, suddenly, someone I did know. Someone I definitely knew.

Chapman.

He appeared suddenly in front of me, carrying a shopping bag from one of the department stores, and heading toward the B. Dalton bookstore.

Chapman! If this dust creature was linked to the Yeerks, he would know. Chapman was our assistant principal at school. He was also one of the highest-ranking Controllers. The slug who lived inside his brain was an important Yeerk.

Chapman would know. Following him had to be more useful than just wandering around the mall. But how? Morphing in a crowded mall would be dangerous.

So what? I reproached myself.

So don't do something stupid just to prove you aren't scared, I argued with myself.

While I was debating with myself, I fell into step a few yards behind Chapman. I had already made up my mind. I just had to decide how I was going to spy on him.

Housefly. Yes. That was the thing. A quick morph, hook on to Chapman, and stay with him for as long as I could remain in morph.

Chapman was in the bookstore, thumbing through magazines. How long would he stay in the bookstore? Long enough? Maybe. And where could I morph without being seen?

I went to the back of the store. There was a storeroom with the door ajar. Inside the storeroom was a second door. A bathroom for the employees. Bingo.

I glanced at Chapman. He had moved to the history section. What on Earth did a Controller want with history?

I swallowed hard and slid into the storeroom, acting like I belonged, but also moving quickly. No one was around. I went into the tiny employees' bathroom and locked the door. I took off my shoes and outer-clothing and stashed them in the trash under a lot of wadded-up paper towels. I would have to come back for them later.

Then I focused. It wasn't easy, because my heart was pounding. And I really didn't like insect morphs much.

I focused on the fly and prayed no one broke

into the bathroom. I felt giddy. I wasn't afraid. Not too afraid, anyway. Even Rachel would have been impressed.

I began to shrink.

It's very weird when you morph into something tiny. One minute your head is like four feet above the floor. Then, suddenly, your head is only two feet above the floor. Then one foot. Six inches. One inch.

It's like falling. And it seems like the floor is rushing up to slap you. I mean, that linoleum seemed to be alive, the way it swooped up at me. It was like being a sky diver spiraling down to Earth.

But there were other very disturbing things happening, too. There is nothing human about a housefly. Everything has to change. Everything.

My hands began to split open. Two of my fingers grew out and became sharp claws. Two other fingers and my thumb blossomed open, splitting into thousands of tiny, sticky hairs.

It's the kind of thing that used to scare me to death when we first started morphing. Let me tell you: The worst horror movie you ever saw in your life is a joke, compared to actually watching your own body turn into something else.

Morphing is almost never pretty. The others all say I'm the best morpher, that I can make it look okay. But nothing can make a fly look okay.

There are no Brad Pitt flies. Flies are ugly-looking creatures — nasty, ugly, gross, disgusting creatures.

My legs were shriveling down and turning into fly legs.

Sploot! Two new legs exploded from my chest, just at the bottom of where my ribs had been. The legs shot out of me like huge black worms. They grew daggerlike hairs and formed joints, and became as hard as plastic.

And my face . . . well, that was definitely unpleasant.

My nose split open, forming two halves. Each half began sprouting long, sensitive hairs. My mouth and tongue melted together, then grew huge, forming a long tube with an open, spitting, sucking hole on the end.

My eyes seemed to shatter, like a mirror broken into a thousand pieces. My vision was gone for a moment, and I was blind. Then it came back, but was so different I almost didn't realize it was sight at all.

I had gone from human eye to compound eye. Where once my vision was a single picture, now it was a thousand bits. It was like watching TV with your nose right against the screen while you twist the color-control knobs. The bits formed pictures, but the colors were all wrong.

At last, I was done morphing. I was a fly. It is

true, I guess, that I am a little faster at morphing than the others — even Ax. I know it's kind of a stupid thing to be proud of, but I am.

I beat my powerful wings, let go of my grip on the tiny ridges in the linoleum, and escaped from the bathroom by zooming neatly beneath the crack of the door.

Once out, I shot quickly up for altitude and safety. And headed for Chapman.

CHAPTER 18

Ax

The dust beast carried me up and up. I could feel gravity tugging at me. I could feel momentum as we moved faster and faster. I could see nothing. I could only hear a swirling sound.

We began to slow down. Slower, slower. Stop.

The dust beast hovered. How high up were we? Where were we?

Then . . . a gap opened in the howling wall of dust that enveloped me. I saw the earth below. But not from orbit. We were still in the atmosphere.

That surprised me. What I saw next did not.

It was not a large ship by most standards. It was far smaller than an Andalite Dome ship.

Far smaller than the Yeerk mother ship. It was all black, with two wings like a battle-ax, and a long, sharp, diamond-shaped battle bridge mounted at the front. I knew the ship. It was the Blade ship. The private command ship of Visser Three.

It had dropped its stealth cloak for just a few moments. Silently, a hole appeared in the top of the battle bridge. The dust beast swirled through.

Suddenly, I was falling! SLAM!

I hit a hard surface. My hooves scrabbled to stand up, but I was down on my side. The dust beast had dropped me on a polished, metallic floor.

I stood up. The dust beast hovered above me.

And all around me on all sides stood Hork-Bajir warriors. Each with a Dracon beam leveled and ready to fire.

There must have been ten of them. Two or three would have been plenty.

Once, the Hork-Bajir were a decent, peaceful race. Then they were enslaved by the Yeerks. Hork-Bajir are incredibly dangerous and very powerful. They stand on two legs, balanced by a tail. Each leg ends in a foot, like an Earth bird of prey. They have two arms. There are curved blades at their knees, at their elbows, at their wrists. Blades similar to my own tail-blade. Atop their snakelike heads are two more blades, swept forward. And their tails end in long, sharp spikes.

They are not a species you want to start a fight with. Which may be why they were such a peaceful, even poetic, species. They had no one to fear. Until the Yeerks began to make them into Controllers.

Now there are no longer any free Hork-Bajir. All are slaves of the Yeerks. All are Controllers, with a living Yeerk inside their brains.

Two or three would have been more than enough to deal with me. Having ten there was a compliment.

<Well, well,> a voice said in my head. <So we have our first captive.>

It was him. As I had known it would be.

Visser Three. Third most powerful of all the Yeerk warlords. The leader of the Yeerk invasion of Earth.

An abomination!

Visser Three is unique in all the galaxy: the one and only Andalite-Controller. He alone, of all Yeerks, has managed to take and enslave an Andalite body.

The sight of him filled me with loathing. My brother's killer! The creature I knew I had to destroy. If I didn't, I would never have the honor of being a true warrior.

I had faced him before. But always with my

human friends beside me. To have attacked the Visser then would have meant risking them.

But now I didn't have that excuse. Visser Three was before me. My brother's killer.

Visser Three focused his main eyes on me. His stalk eyes watched the dust beast as it hovered uneasily above our heads.

I am ashamed to confess it, but I felt terror in his presence. Evil radiated from him. And power. A great and frightening power.

<You're not even full-grown, Andalite,> Visser Three sneered. <My *Veleek* brings me a child?>

<*Veleek?*> I said.

<Yes. I named it myself. In the Yeerk language it means "pet." It's a rare life-form from right here in this solar system. The big gas giant, the one with the very prominent rings.>

Saturn. That's what the humans called it. But I said nothing to the Visser. Answering might have revealed that I was in contact with humans.

Visser Three considered me. <So, you *are* an Andalite, after all. Some of my advisers have been suggesting you terrorists were human, not Andalite. But here we have a prime Andalite specimen.>

The Yeerks believed the Animorphs were a group of Andalites who had survived the battle in orbit and made it to Earth. It was important for them to go on believing it.

<Yeerk filth!> I cried suddenly. <My uncles will destroy you!>

Visser Three laughed. <You and your "uncles" have caused me some annoyance, it is true. You destroyed the truck ship we used to gather oxygen and water. That was very unfortunate. And you destroyed our ground-based Kandrona. That was even more unfortunate.> He stepped closer, showing his complete confidence. Showing me that he did not fear me. <For that, I will give you a very, very long, very slow death, Andalite.>

I wanted to strike at him. My brother . . . Prince Elfangor . . . he would have had the courage. But I did not. The Hork-Bajir would have disintegrated me before I could twitch my tail. And the awful force of the Yeerk Visser's power held me mesmerized.

<Yes, you led me a chase, you Andalite bandits,> Visser Three said. <But my *Veleek* will capture you, one by one, and bring you to me.>

If I lacked the courage to attack and die, I could at least try to learn more. If I lived . . . if I escaped somehow, by some miracle . . .

<How do you make a Controller out of something made of dust? Where do you place your filthy slug body?>

<Oh, the *Veleek* is not one of us,> Visser Three said. <He is not a Controller. He's not really "he." There is no intelligence there — or at

least not much. Fascinating life-form, really. Unlike anything we've ever found before. It spreads through the atmosphere as a dust. Each particle can sense life-form energy — any life-form. When one particle senses prey, the millions of particles come together to attack the life-form and chew it into shreds. The energy of each shredded bit is then absorbed by the particles themselves.>

Visser Three laughed again, soundless, but vile in my mind. <We lost a lot of soldiers before we figured the creature out. Oh, yes. It was chewing up Hork-Bajir and Taxxons at a startling rate. But then we realized something — it could be altered. We could use the thing. I could program it to serve me.>

I nodded, understanding the truth. <You changed it to detect only the energy of morphing.>

<Very good. But you Andalites always have been clever when it comes to science. Yes, now it detects only the specific type of energy released during morphing. But it cannot feed on that energy. Oh, no, no. I didn't want it to *shred* you Andalites. I didn't want it to eat you. I wanted to have you here. With me. So I programmed my *Veleek* to eat only the energy we feed it from the engines of this ship. Clever, isn't it? The *Veleek* senses morphing, attacks, but brings the morpher to me in order to get its true food.>

<Only a Yeerk would think it clever to force mutation on another life-form,> I said, as contemptuously as I could. Should I strike? *Could* I strike? Was I fast enough?

Visser Three nodded. <Yes, yes. We lowly Yeerks know how superior you Andalites are. Holier-than-thou. The meddling moralists of the galaxy. The glorious, self-righteous Andalite princes, saving the galaxy from the despised Yeerks. Well. Here you are, Andalite child. And soon the rest of your group of bandits will be here as well. How many of you are there, all together?>

<I'll tell you nothing,> I said.

<It doesn't matter,> Visser Three said with cold disdain. <The *Veleek* will never tire. I'll send it back and it will go on hunting. Your friends will be clever. Sometimes they will escape — for a while. But sooner or later, my *Veleek* will hunt them down and, one by one, bring them to me.>

He jerked his hand in a signal to his soldiers. <Throw him to the cage. Watch him. If he escapes, each of you will die. Oh, and have the *Veleek* fed, then release it. Let it go to find me more Andalites. I wouldn't want our young Andalite to be lonely.>

The Hork-Bajir grabbed me roughly. Visser Three turned his back and walked away.

I had not struck. I had been face-to-face with my brother's killer, and I had let him walk away.

CHAPTER 19

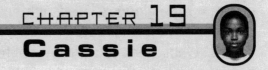

Cassie

ZOOOOM! I beat my fly wings and zipped under the door. The bottom edge of the door was like a ceiling to me, and then I was out.

ZOOOOM! I flew straight up. I mean, straight up. Like a rocket.

<Cool!> I yelled to no one.

ZOOOOM! I spun around in midair and hit the ceiling with all six feet. The long claws dug into tiny cracks in the ceiling tile. The sticky pads added extra hold. I rested upside down, hanging from the ceiling.

Becoming a fly is disgustingly gross. But *being* a fly is excellent. I mean, nothing flies like a housefly! You can fly straight ahead, or you can suddenly shoot straight up, or you can stop and just hover. There is absolutely nothing those fly wings won't do. The best jet fighter, flown by the greatest pilot ever, is a big, slow, wallowing pig compared to a housefly. Tobias on his best day couldn't come close to the maneuvers a fly can do.

I rested on the ceiling, directly above Chapman's head. It was maybe five feet from me down to his balding head. At least, I think it was him. Fly eyesight is hard to get used to. *Very* hard to get used to. Fortunately he — or at least the guy I *hoped* was Chapman — had stepped in some dog doo earlier. I wasn't sure of my weird compound eyesight. But nothing can smell poop like a fly. I was locked onto the location of Chapman's shoe.

There was just one problem: Chapman wasn't doing anything but looking at books. My fly brain got edgy just staying in one place, so I dropped from the ceiling, pivoted in midair, fired up my wings, and took a quick, wild ride around his head.

Yes. It was Chapman. Almost for sure.

For the next twenty minutes I just stalked him on his slow progress through the bookstore. I zipped around him, always staying out of reach, occasionally resting on the spine of a book or rocketing back up to the ceiling.

After twenty minutes or so, it was all starting to look like a pretty stupid idea. I was supposed to be looking for Rachel, who might be in some kind of trouble. And instead I was staring upside down at Chapman's scalp.

Then . . . yes! A man and a woman were talking to Chapman.

Understanding speech is difficult, with the hearing flies have available. Fortunately, I had been a fly before. So I knew how to translate the vibrations the fly felt into "sound."

"You're late," Chapman snapped.

The man said, "It couldn't be helped. Our job isn't easy, with all this going on."

"Not here," Chapman said. "Walk with me."

He walked away, and the two newcomers fell into step alongside him. I dropped from the ceiling, and buzzed quickly after them. It was easy to keep up. I just kept Chapman's head a few feet in front of me. What was hard was hearing everything they said. Out in the mall itself there was a din of noise. Dozens of voices, music, footsteps — it was all vibrations to my antennae and hairs.

To make sense of it, I had to take a risk. I shot forward at full speed, pivoted sideways, and landed on Chapman's collar. The threads of his shirt fabric looked as big as ropes to me. It was easy to hold on. But I kept my fly instincts hyperalert in case some big human hand came reaching to swat me.

"I don't see why we're meeting like this," the woman said. "It's a little melodramatic, isn't it? Like some stupid human spy novel."

"Visser Three does not trust our communications lately. Visser One has supporters among some of our people here. Don't forget — our leader trapped these Andalites once before, and they were freed by Visser One to embarrass us."

"Has that been proven?" the man asked.

Chapman snorted derisively. "If it had been proven, Visser One would be screaming in the torture chambers of the Council of Thirteen. But we know it, just the same. Visser Three isn't going to let anything get in the way this time. This new creature of his, this *Veleek*, will finish the terrorists once and for all."

Veleek, I thought. *The enemy had a name.*

"And make a huge mess doing it," the woman grumbled. "I've been running around all day, trying to keep this story covered up."

"That's why you've been placed on the police force," Chapman said coldly. "It's your job to control police investigations that could be . . . difficult . . . for us."

"There's only one of me," the woman said, not intimidated at all by Chapman's tone. "Ten percent of the police force are our people. But that leaves ninety percent who are human. And the humans are not complete idiots. We have witnesses talking about monsters made of dust, not tornadoes."

"It's the same at the newspaper," the man said. "So far, this story is under control. People believe the tornado nonsense. But you have to tell Visser Three to —"

Suddenly, I was swung wildly around. I released the collar and flew upward. Chapman had stopped, jerked around, and grabbed the man's arm. Chapman had his face an inch from the man's face.

"Tell Visser Three? *Tell* Visser Three? No one tells Visser Three. People who tell the Visser something he doesn't want to hear end up cut off from Kandrona rays, slowly starving, dying inside their hosts. With the rationing of Kandrona rays since the bandits destroyed the Earth-based Kandrona, the Visser has been looking for excuses to eliminate hungry Yeerks. Now, if you want to go *tell* the Visser not to use his *Veleek*, you go right ahead."

He released the man and they all started walking again.

"*Veleek*," the woman grumbled. "Do we have to rely on such things to track down a handful of Andalite terrorists?"

"Yes," Chapman said. "And be glad the Visser has his 'morph-hunter.' It distracts him from asking why you haven't caught the Andalites. You'd better hope this dust creature succeeds. The pressure is building on the Visser to clean up this mess on Earth. There is talk he may be demoted to Visser Four. Even Five. If Visser Three loses rank because of your failure, take my advice: Kill yourselves. Don't wait for the Visser to do it for you."

The two newcomers fell silent after that.

Chapman gave them some instructions. Mostly to just stick to the tornado story, no matter what happened. He told them humans were fools who would believe any sort of nonsense. And if any witnesses became too troublesome, they should be eliminated or made into Controllers.

It was a chilling conversation to hear. And there was nothing in it about Rachel. But just the same, I had learned something important.

The *Veleek was* a tool of Visser Three's.

And they had called it a "morph-hunter."

It was time to head back to the little bathroom and demorph. I needed to talk to Jake and the others. Immediately.

Morph-hunter.

It had struck Marco and Ax when they were demorphing in the basement of Darlene's house. It had almost killed them.

Had it succeeded with Rachel?

CHAPTER 20

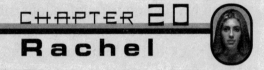

Rachel

I think the pain would have killed me, if I had been human. But I was not just human. I was the bear. And because of the bear's strength, I held on.

My front paws were gone. Chewed off by the terrible dust monster. Blood was everywhere. I could not walk like a bear. But I could wallow along on two legs, until I had gotten far enough away from the terrifying creature.

I found a stream, no more than a foot deep and three feet wide. I sank down into the water and tried to change.

I didn't know if I could. I didn't know how I had become a bear. So I wasn't sure if I could become human again. And if I did . . . what about my hands? Did this terrible injury to my bear body mean that my human hands would be gone, too?

Rachel. That's what the other creature had called me. The creature that looked like a deer and a scorpion and a boy. He'd made no sound, but I had heard his voice in my head. He'd called me "Rachel."

Was I Rachel?

I focused on becoming human again. But all the time, I braced myself for pain beyond endurance.

I lay on my side in the stream. Cold water bubbled and rushed around me. I kept the stumps of my paws in the numbing water. And slowly, I grew smaller. Smaller and weaker. I held the bloody stumps up so I could see them. I would have cried, if I'd had human tears. Fingers . . . human fingers . . . were growing from the gore.

My hands grew back. The carpet of rough fur was replaced by skin and the black fabric of my leotard. Massive bear legs became my own human limbs. My sense of smell grew weak, as my sense of sight grew strong.

I stood up. Shaky. Weak. But no longer in pain. And what was strange was that the scratches and scrapes I'd gotten from walking barefoot through the woods were gone. I was renewed.

I looked fearfully around for the dust beast, but I saw nothing. It was growing dark. Would darkness protect me? Or would it help my enemy?

I looked closer, searching for the alien who knew my name.

Alien?

The word stuck in my mind. Yes! Yes, that creature could not have been from Earth. I knew that. Those memories were still intact. I didn't know whether I knew the alien, or whether he was good or evil, but he *had* to be an alien.

Like the dust beast. Yes. Yes, of course. The old woman ranting about "Yeerks." They were aliens, weren't they?

FLASH! A construction site. Half-finished buildings all around. Heavy equipment. Dark night. A light in the sky. Something . . . landing. Something . . . *alien.* People around me. Faces. Faces I knew . . .

"What faces?" I cried. But the vision was gone.

"Arrrrggghhh!" I yelled in frustration. I wanted to kick something. I wanted to reach inside my own head and tear down the gray curtain that hid the truth from me.

Get a grip, Rachel, I told myself. *At least you know your name. And you know that you have some very weird powers. And you know you have some very serious enemies.*

This was not reassuring. The dust beast would have destroyed me. Except he'd been distracted. By the alien.

Was the alien a friend? Had he been trying to help me?

The answers aren't here in the forest, I told myself. *You need to get back to civilization. That's where the answers are.*

Back to the world. But which direction? The bear would know. He would have been able to sense it. Could I do the same?

I stood very still. I listened.

The wind rustled the leaves. Squirrels chattered. Things I couldn't see skittered behind bushes. Birds sang songs of love and threat. The stream chuckled over rocks and fallen branches.

The stream. Of course.

Follow the stream, I told myself.

CHAPTER 21
Marco

<I didn't see *anything*, all right?> Tobias said angrily. <No bear. No Rachel. No Ax. How many more times do you want to ask me? I didn't see them.>

He was in the rafters of Cassie's barn. We sat on bales of hay or paced back and forth, glaring and angry and, worst of all, afraid.

Jake, Cassie, me, and Tobias. Four of the six who should have been there.

"All right, calm down, Tobias," Jake said. "No one is blaming you. No one is blaming anyone. We just need to get a grip on this."

"Ax was supposed to hook up with us in the forest," I said. "He never did. If he couldn't meet us, he'd know we'd worry. He'd know he should morph into his human form and come tell us he's okay."

"So he's *not* okay," Jake said.

"Ax is not okay and Rachel is not okay," I agreed. "And I think we know why. That thing." I turned to Cassie. "What did Chapman call it?"

"A *Veleek*. A morph-hunter."

"That's why Rachel and Ax have both disappeared," I said. "It almost got me and Ax at Darlene's. It almost got us again this afternoon."

Cassie looked at me, her expression troubled. "Why 'almost'?"

"What do you mean?"

"Why *didn't* it get you?" Cassie asked. She was frowning. "At Darlene's house it had you cold. Today, you say you outran it. But actually, it stopped chasing you, right? It went tearing off to the cabin where we think Ax and Rachel were. Why? Why stop chasing you two and go after them?"

"I don't know!" I yelled. I was as frustrated and scared as anyone. I wasn't in the mood for puzzles. "Ask Tobias. He's the predator here. He should know."

I meant it to be mean. I felt bad about it as soon as I said it.

But Tobias didn't lash back at me. Instead he said, <Movement.>

"What's that supposed to mean?" Jake asked.

<Marco said it: I'm a predator. When I hunt, I look for movement. I chase what moves. Same as a cat. If the prey stays still, it's harder to see. If I listen and I don't *hear* movement, it's the same thing. The hawk's brain is wired to pay attention to the sight or sound of movement.>

"That's it!" Cassie yelled.

I jerked about two feet in the air. Cassie is not a person who yells.

"That's it! It's been bugging me ever since the first attack. How did the *Veleek* know who we were? How did it decide Marco and Ax were prey? Marco, what were you doing just as the beast attacked?"

I shrugged. "I was morphing back."

"Yes!" Cassie said. "Coincidence? The beast just happens to attack *while* you are morphing? And today, when you guys were attacked in the woods?"

"We were morphing," Jake said. "We were morphing into wolves."

"Both attacks at the very time you were morphing," Cassie said. "The very time. Interesting coincidence."

We all just pretty much didn't say anything for a few seconds after that. I was trying to think through what this would mean: As long as I didn't morph, I was safe. As safe as a mouse who stays frozen.

"Rachel doesn't know this," I said quietly. "If she's even alive."

"Why did the *Veleek* drop us and take off for the cabin in the woods?" Jake asked. Then he answered his own question. "Because we were done morphing, so we weren't as interesting to it. It sensed some other creature actively morphing."

<Two mice in a field. Maybe I'm chasing one, and he's running. But then he freezes. No movement. And at that moment I catch a glimpse of another mouse running. I . . . or at least the hawk, goes after the second mouse. The hawk brain thinks they're the *same* mouse. What's important is the movement.>

"And for this morph-hunter, what counts is the morphing. That's what it locks onto," Jake said.

"So why didn't it come after me when I morphed at the mall?" Cassie wondered.

"Because it can't be two places at once," I said. "There must be limits on how far it can spread. It was too far away."

"We're safe, as long as we never morph again," I pointed out.

"You mean as long as we don't fight the Yeerks, we're safe," Jake said. "Is that what you think we should do, Marco?"

They all looked at me. I shrugged. "Rachel

isn't here to cast her vote. So, on her behalf, I'll say what she would say: What we need to do is find a way to kick this *Veleek*'s butt."

Cassie smiled. "And what would the real Marco say to that?"

"He'd probably make some stupid but very funny remark," I admitted. "Then he would start thinking about how to do just that: Kick this big windbag's dusty butt."

CHAPTER 22
Rachel

I reached civilization. Or at least, I reached a suburban development. Maybe it was familiar, I don't know. Maybe I'd been there before. I didn't know that, either.

What I did know was that my feet were scratched and torn. My legs were aching and sore. My entire body was sore. I was hungry and thirsty and scared. And I was tired beyond belief.

I needed sleep. I could see lights on inside many of the homes I passed. For a while I considered just walking right up to the front door of any house and saying, "Look, I don't know who I am. Can I sleep on your couch?"

But I was being hunted by someone, or something. I didn't know who I could trust. And until my memory returned, I had to be cautious. Besides, I was dirty, messed-up, barefoot, and wearing a stupid black leotard. No one was going to let me in.

Then I saw the house with no lights on inside. There was a sign on the front lawn that said SOLD. I crossed the damp lawn, which felt wonderful to my sore feet. I peered in through a front window. No furniture. It was empty.

I quickly went around to the back. The house had a pool. And I saw a faucet down behind some bushes. I fell to my knees and turned the knob till cool, fresh water flowed. I drank my fill.

"Well, that's one thing taken care of," I whispered to myself.

I checked out the houses on either side. There was a high fence all the way around. No one could see me.

I tried the back door: locked. I tried the garage door: locked. Then I tried a window. Yes!

I hoisted myself up and slid inside. It was dark. The house smelled like fresh paint. "Is anyone here?" I called out in a trembly voice.

My voice fell flat in the emptiness. I went to the kitchen and opened the refrigerator. The light surprised me. Inside the refrigerator was nothing.

I checked the cupboards. Empty. Empty. Empty. Ah-hah! Right there on the counter: a box of Nilla Wafers. They must have belonged to the painters. There were paint fingerprints on the box. It was open, and half the cookies were gone, but I didn't care. I wolfed the cookies down as I prowled through the rest of the empty house.

The place was empty, but I had water and cookies, and the carpet was soft enough to sleep on, as tired as I was.

I sat in a corner of the abandoned living room and finished eating the cookies. I wondered who had lived here. And who would be moving in next.

But most of all, I wondered about me. Who I was. *What* I was. And why some terrible alien creature had tried to kill me twice.

I don't remember falling asleep. But later I remembered the dreams. The nightmares.

FLASH! I was at the construction site. Dark. A light coming down from the sky. Others with me. Was one a girl? Yes. But I couldn't see her face. Or the faces of others with me. Just one . . . a boy . . . He turned to look at me.

A bird! He had the face of a bird of prey.

FLASH! I was balancing. Putting one foot carefully in front of another. I was on a beam. Four inches wide. I felt clumsy. But when I looked down at my feet, they changed. They weren't my feet at all, but the dainty paws of a cat.

People applauding. No, not all. Some hated me. Wanted to kill me. Something wrong with them. Something terribly wrong with them! Worms! Worms in their heads!

FLASH! I was underground. A vast open pit, but covered by a dome of rock and dirt. A pool of sluggish gray water. The worms! They were in the water. And all around me . . . blades everywhere, heads like snakes.

Huge ants! No, no, I was an ant, too. Reeking acid smells. Hundreds of them swarming, attacking. Ants as big as I was. Huge pincers cutting into me.

Morph back! I cried in my dream.

Morph back!

Morph!

"ANIMORPH!" I woke up screaming.

I jumped up off the floor. I ran my hands frantically over my body. What was I? What *was* I? What was I that I had these dreams?

Humans did not dream of being ants. Dreams that were so real you could feel the huge grains of sand pressing in, the airlessness, the terror, the eerie vision of swarms of ants crawling over you, ripping you apart.

I was gasping for breath. My heart was beating twice its normal rate. My forehead was dripping sweat, even though it was chilly in the empty room.

Animorph. That's what I had screamed. What did it mean?

Then . . .

BAM BAM BAM!

"Whoever is in there, come out. This is the police!"

"Ahh!" I yelped, then covered my mouth. Flashlight beams pierced the darkness around me. Spears of light searched for me. I rolled quickly into a corner.

"Don't make us come in there after you!" a policeman said. "Neighbors reported someone climbing in. So just come on out."

Trapped! I should just . . . I should just give myself up.

No! No! There were enemies. Enemies everywhere. I couldn't . . . I couldn't . . .

"I'm gonna count to three and you'd better come out with your hands over your head," a policeman yelled.

I had to get away! Had to think. Had to find out who I was. What I was. But I was surrounded.

Morph! Like when I became a bear. Only not the bear. I didn't know if the bear inside me was injured.

I searched the jagged memories from my dreams. What had I seen? What pictures had I seen? The ant? NO! Never the ant. Never again. I felt that in my bones.

Larger. More powerful. Yes!

The cops were banging and yelling. My skin was still electric from the terrifying nightmares. But I calmed myself. I focused on one image from my dreams.

Large. Very large. Too large for the police to handle.

"Ohhh!" I cried out as my nose and upper lip suddenly exploded outward. Exploded in a long, massive growth that reached to the floor.

I was growing larger. Larger. Filling the room!

"Come out of there now, or we're coming in!"

Don't worry, officer, I thought. *I'll be out soon.*

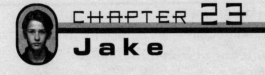

CHAPTER 23
Jake

It was just dumb luck that we even saw what happened.

Our meeting broke up with all of us mad and scared and upset. No one wanted to believe that Rachel and Ax might have been killed. Ax was a new friend, sort of. And an alien, not someone we had grown up with. But Rachel was my cousin. She was Cassie's best friend. And we looked up to Rachel. She was fearless. She made the rest of us braver than we might have been without her.

We went out into the night, the four of us. Tobias flew off toward the forest. We watched him fly away, flapping hard in the dead night air. Marco and I picked up our bikes.

"Cassie? Are you out there?" It was her mother, framed in the doorway of their home.

"Yes, Mom. Right here."

"That show you like is on. Do you want me to tape it?"

"I'll be in in a minute," Cassie said. "I'm just talking to Jake and Marco."

"Hi, Jake. Hello, Marco."

We said hello back.

"Well, don't stay out too late," Cassie's mom said. "It's almost nine o'clock." She went back inside.

"Nine? Man, I better be getting home," Marco said. "I'll be toast."

"I'll walk you guys to the road," Cassie said. We walked in silence down the long driveway, then down the dirt road that connected the farm to the highway. Marco and I pushed our bikes, and the only sounds were our footsteps and the rattle of Marco's balky bike chain.

"Maybe she's home already. Maybe we don't even have to worry," I said. "And Ax is probably fine. I mean, who knows what an Andalite might be doing?"

"At least it's warm out," Cassie said. "If Rachel is out there somewhere, at least it's a warm night. And there's a bright moon to help her find her way home," she added softly.

I followed her gaze. The full moon hung high

in the sky, surrounded by millions of stars. You can always see a lot more stars out on Cassie's farm.

"Look!" Marco yelled.

Something was obscuring the moon. It passed swiftly and the moon shone clear again. I saw what looked like sparkling fairy dust. A swirl that raced away toward the development whose lights were just visible in the middle distance.

"What is that? Is that a cloud?" Cassie asked.

I looked at her. "I don't think so."

"You *know* what it is," Marco snapped. "What are we going to do about it?"

"Morph-hunter," Cassie said. "It's after someone. Ax. Or Rachel."

"Two choices," I said. "Do nothing. Or try and distract it."

"Distract it?" Marco demanded. "How?"

"Like playing keepaway," I said. "It chases morphs, right? So we give it something to chase."

"We have to get it away from those houses," Cassie said. "That thing chews up everything in its path!"

Marco nodded. "Keep shifting targets. Keep it guessing. Oh, man! This is going to be really unpleasant!"

"How do we get there?" Cassie demanded. "We can't morph here and fly over. If we morph here we'll draw it to my house!"

She was right. And the houses where the *Veleek* was headed were half a mile away.

"Are the keys in that?" Marco asked.

Cassie and I looked where he was pointing. Cassie's father's beat-up old pickup truck. The truck he used around the farm.

"No way," Cassie said.

"Way," Marco said.

Which left it up to me to decide. "Let's do it."

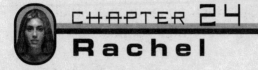

CHAPTER 24
Rachel

I had become very, very large.

The cops were still outside pounding and yelling and ordering me to come out.

So I decided I'd better do what they wanted.

I aimed for the front door. Not that the front door was going to be big enough. But I figured the front *wall* would be just about big enough. I could feel the morph progressing. In a minute now, as soon as the morph was complete —

B-R-R-A-A-A-A-K-K!

Behind me some terrible noise! Noise like a circular saw going through steel!

"HhhhREEEEEuuuhhh!" I trumpeted in terror and rage.

B-R-R-A-A-A-A-K-K!

Suddenly, the back wall of the house was gone! The beast! The beast!

Head down, trunk curled under, I charged the front door.

KaaaaaRUNCH!

I hit the front door. The door popped out like a champagne cork. The frame around the door exploded into splinters. Then the wall around the door frame bulged out and popped open like a pimple.

And out I came. Several tons of me. An insane, horrific combination of human and African elephant. The unpredictability of the incomplete morph had resulted in a huge creature with a long trunk, tiny, human ears, big elephant legs, and blond hair.

The police officers were surprised.

"HhhhRRRRRRuuuhhh!" I trumpeted again. I raised my massive trunk high in the air. Four police officers stared with identical expressions of total, absolute disbelief. Four mouths hung open. They blinked. One of them rubbed her eyes.

Then they had something even more amazing to see.

The dust creature ripped through the house, just a few feet behind me, leaving it a mess of chopsticks. I bolted.

You would not think, to look at an elephant,

that it can even run at all. But believe me, an elephant can move out when it needs to. Elephants can go twenty-five miles an hour, faster than the fastest human runner.

But there is a problem with elephants, too. They are huge. Too huge to dodge and twist. Too huge to hide.

I barreled down that quiet suburban street, completing the morph as I ran. But I knew I could not escape.

BLAM! BLAM! BLAM! BLAM!

The police were shooting! At me? At the dust monster? I didn't know. I didn't care. The bullets meant nothing to me, and nothing to the monster that was after me.

It was after me! A hundred feet back, a huge, flying wall of gnashing teeth and whirring blades.

It was gaining!

I stomped through someone's garden, crushed flowers beneath my huge, round feet, and annihilated a fence. I turned toward an alleyway between two homes. A parked Winnebago was between me and the beast.

B-R-R-A-A-A-A-K-K!

The Winnebago was gone! Out of the corner of my eye, I saw a single tire bounce down the street. The rest of the camper was shredded.

Right then, I knew it was over. If I kept running, the beast would chew its way through houses where innocent people were sleeping. I couldn't let that happen.

This is it, I realized. *This is it. I can't run. I can't win.* I turned to face the beast.

I saw it slow down. It hung in the air before me. A nightmare of gnashing teeth and wild eyes and whirling blades. The last of the morph was completed, as two gigantic ivory tusks sprouted from my mouth.

From the beast, tendrils emerged. They were like ropes. Living ropes that wrapped around my huge body.

I felt myself being smothered. I couldn't breathe!

I struggled, but the ropes just tightened their grip. The dust beast swirled around me, covering me.

I couldn't see. I could barely breathe.

Then the beast lifted me up.

Or . . . it tried to.

I felt myself raised up, up . . . maybe a foot off the ground. Then we settled back to Earth.

Once again, the beast tried to lift me. This time we rose two, maybe three feet.

And then settled down to Earth again.

At that moment, a tiny flicker of hope was reborn.

I looked it up in a book once — the largest elephant ever found weighed 22,050 pounds.

Mostly they weigh in between 7,000 and 13,000 pounds. I had no idea how much I weighed in this elephant body. Probably not 22,050 pounds. But I was big, just the same. Very big.

Too big for the dust beast to carry away.

<Heh, heh, heh. Too much for you, creep?>

Penetrating the swirling, angry sounds of the dust beast as it strained to lift me up came a sudden SCCRREEEEEECHH! It sounded like squealing tires. Like a very bad driver was racing toward us.

CHAPTER 25

Marco

"Aaaaaaaahhhhh!" Cassie screamed.

"Look out! Lookoutlookoutlookoutlookout!" Jake yelled.

"Would you both shut up?" I demanded. "I'm trying to drive here!"

"Car! Car! Car!" Jake yelled.

I yanked the wheel left. The car sped by, horn blaring. The driver stuck his hand out the window and made a sign with his fingers.

"That's rude," I said. "And totally uncalled for."

BAM!

"Aaaaaaaahhhhhh!"

"Oh, it's just a trash can," I said. "Chill out."

BAM! BAM! BAM!

"Okay, so it's four trash cans," I said.

"Get off the sidewalk, you lunatic!" Jake said.

I yanked the wheel to the right. We bumped off the sidewalk, sort of grazed a parked car, and . . .

BAM! BAM! BAM!

"Do you hate trash cans?" Jake asked. "Is that your problem? Do you just HATE TRASH CANS?!!"

"I can't drive with you screaming in my ear," I said.

"You can't drive at all!" Jake said.

"Left! Turn left! There, there! Turn left! It's that way," Cassie said, taking time out from screaming.

I turned left. I missed the actual street, but fortunately, the people who lived on that corner did not have any trees in their front yard.

BUMP! Over the curb. BUMP! Rear wheels over the curb. I stepped on the gas and tore across the lawn.

"Cool," I said.

"I'm going to kill you, Marco," Jake said in a weirdly calm voice. "If I survive, I am gonna kill you."

"You said you could drive!" Cassie accused.

I shrugged. Actually, what I had said was I

scored millions of points playing Wipeout, this excellent video game. "Okay, so it's not exactly like Wipeout. I'm doing the best I can."

BUMP. BUMP. I was back on the road.

Suddenly, an elephant went tearing across the street a block away. An elephant with little pink ears.

The *Veleek* was right behind it.

"That's Rachel!" Cassie yelled. "She's still alive!"

"Not for long, maybe," Jake said grimly. "I'm gonna morph. Marco? Follow that elephant!"

The elephant ran behind a Winnebago. The *Veleek* chewed the Winnebago into sawdust.

The elephant turned to face the animal. The elephant planted its feet firmly, raised its trunk in defiance, and faced the beast of a hundred mouths.

"Yeah, that's Rachel, all right," I said.

I floored the truck. We burned rubber and shot forward down the block.

"Come on, you big dirtball, I'm right here!" Jake yelled. Orange and black fur was already sprouting from his body. Tiger teeth were growing, bulging down beneath his upper lip.

Suddenly, living ropes, like tentacles, wrapped around Rachel's huge body. The dust beast enveloped her. Covered her.

"NO!" Cassie cried. "Rachel! NO!"

The *Veleek* began to rise from the ground.

Then it slipped back down.

"Oh! Duh!" I gasped. "It's not trying to *kill* us! It wants to *capture* us! It's trying to carry Rachel away."

"It can't lift her," Cassie said. "She's too heavy."

Just then, the *Veleek* noticed us. Or at least it noticed Jake, who was morphing into a tiger.

The *Veleek* dropped Rachel. She fell just a foot or so, but still cracked the road surface.

"I'm going to Rachel," Cassie yelled. She started climbing over Jake to get out. But it wasn't working because Jake was already half-tiger, and he was squeezing out of his seat.

"Jake, better climb in the back, man. You're getting large," I said and put on the brakes.

Jake pushed open the door and climbed out of the truck. He was clumsy because he had legs that were not human and not tiger, but some weird halfway mix. His hands were fur-covered claws that could barely work the door handle.

But Jake piled out and jumped into the back of the pickup. Cassie piled out right behind him.

"Good luck, you guys," Cassie said. She slammed the door shut.

With a rush of wind, the *Veleek* came after us.

I put the truck in reverse and gunned it.

WHAM!

I groaned. Someone had parked a car right where I needed to go.

<Turn it around!> Jake yelled in thought-speak.

I spun the wheel and at the same time I floored it. It was totally Hollywood! We're talking squealing tires, smoke coming up off them, then ZOOOOM!

I had a tiger in the back of a pickup truck I could barely drive, and I was being chased by the most powerful monster I had ever seen.

Later I would be terrified. But right then, at that moment, I was just thinking, *This is so cool.*

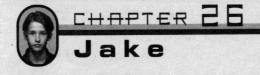

CHAPTER 26
Jake

The good news was Marco had gotten out of the neighborhood, so he couldn't destroy any more trash cans.

The bad news was he'd gotten onto the highway.

<Pass on the left, pass on the left! Not on the right!>

"Hey, I'm cool now," Marco yelled back through the open back window of the truck. "This is just like the game now. No problem-o."

<It isn't dark on the video game.>

"Sure. The part with the tunnel."

<You mean the part where you always crash and burn?>

We were tearing down the highway at seventy

miles an hour, weaving through a stream of bright red taillights. I was halfway into the tiger morph. I was deliberately dragging it out, keeping the *Veleek* interested.

It was working. The *Veleek* was interested.

I was standing in the rattling, swaying bed of a junky old pickup truck, and just about five carlengths back there was a beast fifty feet wide that was nothing but sheer destruction.

Occasionally, the other motorists on the road would offer us advice. I could hear bits and pieces of it as we shot past.

". . . idiots! Why don't you . . ."

"What kind of a moron . . ."

"Where'd you learn to drive? Jersey? You stupid . . ."

<It's gaining on us!> I told Marco.

"This thing won't go any faster!"

<Good,> I said.

"Off-road! We're going off-road!"

<Nooooo!>

But it was too late.

Ka-BUMPH! Bump! Bumpbumpbumpbumpbump!

The truck plunged off the road, jumped a ditch, slammed through a wire fence, and aimed straight for the trees.

Tree left! Tree right! Tree! Tree! Tree! Tree!

Branches scraped at the sides of the truck.

And behind us, chewing through the trees, came the *Veleek.*

B-R-R-A-A-A-A-A-K-K!

<Marco, I'm almost morphed. I'm gonna bail. Give me five minutes, then it's your turn.>

"Yeah," Marco yelled. "Jake? Be careful, man!"

<Try not to destroy Cassie's dad's truck, okay?>

"Get ready. Slowing down . . ."

He slammed on the brakes. WHAM! The side of the truck slid into a tree. I sprang from the bed of the truck. Marco floored the truck and sped off through the brush, engine roaring.

I landed like the cat I was. The tiger inside me knew where we were. Knew it in his bones. This was a cat born and bred for dark nights in dense forests.

In a rush of sensory information, I heard-smelled-saw the environment around me. Dark-penetrating eyes. Ears attuned to every small sound. A sense of smell that told me stories of deer and wolves and wild pigs that had passed through this area.

But what I needed most was the cat's agility and speed. I completed the morph. As long as no one else morphed and distracted it, the *Veleek* would chase me. At least, that's what I hoped.

B-R-R-A-A-A-A-A-K-K!

It was on me! I turned with lightning speed and did the one thing the *Veleek* could not expect: I charged straight at it.

The dust beast hesitated, then stopped.

"RRRROOOOOWWWWRRR!" I let loose a roar that would make a grown man wet his pants. I unleashed the incredible power of my coiled muscles. I leapt through the air, claws outstretched. It was an attack that would kill just about any animal walking around on this planet.

But it would have had no effect on the *Veleek.*

At the last second, before my paws could encounter those rows of gnashing teeth and spinning blades, I tucked my head, drew my paws back, and hit the ground directly beneath the dust beast.

SHWOOOM! Right under him! Right under the *Veleek* and out the far side. I hauled my orange-striped tail out of there at maximum warp.

<Let's see how fast you can turn, creep!>

Hah. Not fast. It took the *Veleek* several seconds to turn itself around. And I thought, *Well, well. So it does have some weaknesses, after all.*

Some weaknesses. Not enough.

B-R-R-A-A-A-A-A-K-K! It ripped through the trees and undergrowth like the out-of-control mulcher it was.

Tigers are fast. Tigers are mightily powerful.

But tigers do not have great endurance. I was a sprinter, not a marathon runner.

I moved out, racing wildly through the trees, turning sharp left, then sharp right. Doubling back. Doubling back again. And the somewhat clumsy *Veleek* couldn't catch me. But I couldn't keep it up. I was winded. Panting. Tongue hanging out. Exhausted. It was time for a distraction. I hoped Marco could provide it in time.

The plan was to run the *Veleek* back and forth, from one morph to another. It wanted to hunt morphs? We would give it morphs to hunt.

It wasn't much of a plan. It only worked if the creature could be worn out.

But the odds were we'd all wear out first.

I fired myself up a tree. Claws bit deep into the bark. Tired muscles propelled me up and up, through the branches.

B-R-R-A-A-A-K!

The *Veleek* chewed through the tree I was on! I looked down and saw it right below me. The tree was still standing, but the *Veleek* had shredded the base. And it was chewing its way straight up the tree.

I leapt into darkness.

I fell, claws outstretched, through the night air.

CHAPTER 27

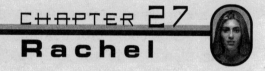

Rachel

The dust beast dropped me. I hit the road. I hit it hard. The concrete cracked and popped open, revealing gravel beneath.

FLASH! I was flying. I was a bird. An eagle. Going to see Tobias. Going to tell him I was going to . . . to what? Something. Birds! Sudden, out of nowhere! Swarming around me. Attacking, in front, the side. Turn, turn and dive to get away! A tree! WHAM!

What? What did it mean? Tobias! I had remembered a name!

I watched the dust beast re-form to go after a truck that was careening backward up the street. Careening straight into a parked car.

Then, a tiger! No, not quite a tiger. Half-human. Half-tiger. A freak! It climbed into the back of the truck.

And someone else was left behind. A girl. Short. Wearing overalls.

FLASH! The construction site. The one where the alien had landed. She was there! *She* was there! I knew this girl. But . . . was she a friend? Or one of them? One of the enemies?

"Rachel!" the girl yelled. "Are you okay?"

Rachel. Yes. What the deer-scorpion-alien had called me at the burning shack. Rachel. Yes. That was my name.

YES! It *was* my name!

FLASH! A woman saying "Rachel, I know you don't like lima beans, eat them anyway, they're good for you."

FLASH! A girl, younger than me, saying, "Rachel, Rachel, Rachel! Everything is always Rachel around here!"

FLASH! A man's voice, from nowhere. "And now, next on the balance beam, Rachel . . ."

YES! I remembered. I was Rachel.

But who was this short girl calling me? And what was I?

"Rachel? Can you hear me?"

<Who are you?> I asked.

"What do you mean, who am I?"

<Who are you?!> I yelled in thought-speak. <Tell me! Tell me, or I'll crush you!>

"Rachel, it's me. Cassie."

Cassie?

"Are you okay?"

<No. I'm not. Are you my friend?>

"Rachel, I've been your friend for years," the girl who called herself Cassie said.

<My memory . . . I don't remember. Cassie? What am I?>

The girl stared at me for a moment. I could see doubt in her eyes. She looked around at the street. The first cops had taken off after the wild pickup truck. But more sirens were blaring, coming closer and closer.

"You're human, Rachel."

<No. I mean, yes, I know. But I'm something else, too. Look at me. How can I do this? What am I?>

Cassie met my gaze. Human to elephant. I guess it seemed bizarre to the frightened, sleepy people who were peeking out of their windows.

"You are an Animorph, Rachel. An Animorph. And I guess something has happened to you to mess up your memory. But right now, my friend, you have to trust me. You *have* to trust me."

Animorph! The word from my dream.

Trust her? Trust this girl who called herself Cassie and said she was my friend? I looked down at her through elephant eyes. Could I trust her? How could I know? How could I be sure?

<Cassie?> I said.

"Yes."

<Tell me what to do.>

CHAPTER 28

Ax

The Yeerks put me in a box. Not a cage, a Ramonite box with seamless walls on all sides.

I was in that box for a time that spanned many Earth hours. And I felt despair. The special despair that comes from dishonor.

Visser Three killed my brother. By the laws and customs of my people, I was supposed to avenge that murder. I was obligated to kill Visser Three, if I ever had the chance.

I had just been face-to-face with him. And I had done nothing. Yes, I had been surrounded by Hork-Bajir. And because I was young and not yet a full-fledged Andalite warrior, I could say that the full burden of revenge had not yet fallen on me.

But it was a bitter feeling. A bitter, terrible

feeling, knowing I had been face-to-face with Visser Three and had not struck. Had I missed my one chance for revenge?

In my mind I pictured the scene again. I had been surrounded by Hork-Bajir, but with Visser Three himself within range of my tail. Could I have struck? Could I have hit him before the Hork-Bajir fired and disintegrated me?

No. Logic said no. But I felt a sick, twisting doubt inside me. Dishonor is a terrible thing. Worse than death for an Andalite warrior.

Suddenly, one wall of my cage shimmered and became transparent. Ramonite is a metal that can stretch open or be made clear or opaque by molecular realignment.

I could see the room beyond my cage: the bridge of Visser Three's Blade ship.

The Visser stood on a raised platform in the center of a triangular room. Aligned on three sides of the bridge were various workstations manned by Taxxons and human-Controllers. Taxxons are wormlike creatures. They have rows of needle-sharp legs, similar to an Earth centipede. They hold the upper third of their bodies erect, and along the upper body, the rows of legs become pairs of weak but agile arms.

A series of globular red eyes surround the top end of the worm. And at the very top is an always-open, circular mouth.

The Hork-Bajir were a race of peace-loving creatures enslaved by the Yeerks. But the Taxxons *chose* to ally themselves with the Yeerks. Each Taxxon now has a Yeerk inside its vile head, adding Yeerk intelligence to the Taxxon's own deep evil.

Taxxons usually handle the more subtle work. Hork-Bajir are used as soldiers. The Yeerk empire was only just beginning to integrate its new human slaves into the empire.

In the air before Visser Three was a hologram. It was obviously being shot from a great distance. The scene was distorted and light-enhanced, which gave it an eerie, dreamlike quality.

<I thought you might enjoy watching this,> Visser Three said to me. <We were lucky to get a visual lock. My *Veleek* is closing in on another of your band. Soon you'll have company.>

The hologram shimmered and wavered, but I could see the *Veleek* tearing through trees in a forest. And then a sudden flash of orange and black. A tiger. Prince Jake!

<There are some magnificent animals on this planet,> Visser Three said. <I'll have to acquire one of those. Look how it moves! But it's wearing out. It's a fast killer. It can't handle the long battle.>

Suddenly, the tiger that was Jake shot up a

tree. The *Veleek* was eating its way up the tree. Prince Jake leapt into the air.

I could just barely see the tiger hit the ground. It bared its teeth, but was too tired to run anymore.

In a second it would be over. The *Veleek* would envelop the tiger and bring it to Visser Three.

Just then, the *Veleek* hesitated. Visser Three stiffened.

The *Veleek* disintegrated and, like a tornado, swept away at extreme speed.

<What is happening?!> Visser Three cried.

Every Taxxon, Hork-Bajir, and human-Controller on the bridge flinched. One of the human-Controllers stepped forward timidly. "Visser, the *Veleek* must have sensed another morph."

<Why doesn't it bring me this one first?>

"Visser, as you know, our knowledge of this *Veleek* is not perfect. I can only speculate. I —"

Suddenly, Visser Three stabbed his tail at the cowering Controller. The blade pressed against the human's throat. <Speculate *quickly*,> Visser Three said.

"It . . . it . . . it . . . Visser, it feeds on energy. It senses energy. We have made it sensitive to the energy field created during morphing. But this bandit . . . this tiger creature has stopped morphing. So the attraction has weakened. The *Veleek* would still capture this tiger, only . . . only some other morph energy field must have been created. The *Veleek* senses this new field and goes after the new energy source."

Visser Three withdrew his tail from the man's neck. The human-Controller collapsed to his knees, sweating and shaking.

<Launch both Bug fighters,> Visser Three said. <Keep a visual lock on the *Veleek*.>

A Taxxon spoke in their strange tongue. "*Sreen yit seewee srinyee sree* —"

Faster than the eye could follow, Visser Three lashed out with his Andalite tail.

"*Skkkrreeeee!*" the Taxxon screamed.

The Taxxon was sliced open! Its insides sloshed out all over the floor. The Taxxon collapsed in a heap.

<This creature says it is difficult to keep a visual lock on the *Veleek*. Does anyone else think it is *difficult* to follow my orders?>

No one did.

<Clean up this incompetent filth. Launch the Bug fighters. Keep a visual lock on the *Veleek*.>

All this was said very calmly. Two Taxxons rushed forward and began to eat their fellow Taxxon. The others on the bridge all paid very close attention to their work.

Very, very close attention.

<I guess it isn't going too well for you, Visser,> I sneered.

He turned his main eyes on me, while his stalk eyes swept the room, looking for any slackness on the part of his creatures.

<Yes, your Andalite brothers have found a weakness in my *Veleek*,> Visser Three said. <They are playing games. Morphing here, morphing there, whipping it from place to place. But you forget, my little Andalite friend: I inhabit an Andalite body with full morphing powers. I know *your* weakness, too. They can't play this game for long. And I am about to add to their troubles.>

He turned all eyes to me in a leering, deadly gaze. <I would like to take them alive, for my own reasons. But if I can't, I will make do with their lifeless bodies.>

CHAPTER 29

Marco

CRRRRUUUUNCHHH! SCRRRREEECH! BAM! WHAM! BUMP! Squuueeeeaall!

Out of the trees I roared, in what was left of the pickup truck. I plowed up through a ditch and onto a road, kicking up dirt and mud and gravel. It was a dark, narrow road that ran behind the housing development. I'd come full circle.

I don't care what anyone says — I drove okay. Or at least I was getting better. I was running into things less, anyway.

I began to morph. But I didn't want to give up on the truck. After all, I was supposed to get it back out to Cassie's farm when we were done with it.

So I chose the one morph I had in my arsenal that could drive.

"Time for the monkey suit," I muttered as I barreled down the road, hitting only the occasional mailbox.

I focused. I concentrated as well as I could. Fortunately, this was a morph I had done before. I was familiar with it.

But still, that first sensation of my shoulders doubling in size . . . tripling . . . quadrupling . . . It was a rush! I mean, I'm not the biggest guy in the world. I'm kind of short. I'm kind of small. But when I do this morph I am so massively powerful it's incredible.

In this morph I have lifted guys up and thrown them through the air. In this morph I have punched Hork-Bajir and they *stayed* punched. In this morph I could kick the butts of the entire Dallas Cowboys all at once.

Four hundred pounds, give or take a few. But not four hundred pounds of fat. No. I was becoming four hundred pounds of hard-core, bad-as-bad-can-be, don't-even-look-cross-eyed-at-me, shoulders like a cement truck, neck like a fire hydrant, fists like sledgehammers, dominant male silverback gorilla.

Sweet, gentle animals . . . unless you insist on making them mad. At which point they are capable of ripping up a small tree by the roots and playing baseball — with you as the ball.

I glanced in the rearview mirror. My eyes had become little gorilla eyes. My mouth was puffing out and turning dark.

And I was scared. See, as tough as my gorilla might be, I was nothing to that dust monster. I wasn't morphing the gorilla to *fight* that thing. I was morphing the gorilla to draw him on.

I was bait.

I was the bait and the creature was the shark. And that fact did not make me happy.

I heard the roar of a tornado behind me.

I pressed my growing foot down on the accelerator.

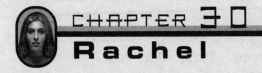

CHAPTER 30

Rachel

I charged with trunk held high, trumpeting defiance. I ran toward the line of trees that hugged the housing development. I crashed heedlessly through yards and lawns. I was in a hurry. And lawns could be fixed.

"Your name is Rachel. You're an Animorph. We were created by a dying Andalite prince. We were given the power to become any animal we could touch."

We were running. Or I was running, anyway, with this girl riding on my back. She told me we had to get away from the homes. We had to get to the forest. The dust beast would kill innocent people if we didn't get away.

That made sense. The rest of what she was telling me seemed utterly insane.

"I'm Cassie. We're best friends, Rachel. There's Jake. He's your cousin. There's Marco. And Tobias. Tobias was trapped in his morph. He's stuck as a —"

FLASH! A terrible place, deep, deep within the bowels of the earth. A dim cave as big as a sports dome. In the center, a pool. A pool that looked like molten lead. Piers reaching into it. Cages around the edges.

The cries! The terrible cries of terror and despair!

A battle raged. I was there. I was there. I was . . .

An elephant! Just as I was now. Yes, a battle against monsters. And a bird screamed down from high in the cave. It screamed down, wings back, hooked beak and terrible talons ready.

<A hawk,> I said to Cassie.

"Yes! Yes! That's it. That's Tobias."

I crashed through a flimsy fence into someone's backyard. Then crashed through it again on my way out. Open field! We were out of the houses now, and running for the cover of the woods.

I remembered what had happened in the woods.

<The old woman was yelling about Yeerks,> I said. <She was crazy. Yelling about Yeerks coming for her.>

"The Yeerks are real," Cassie said. "Look, Rachel, you don't have to remember everything at once. But we're in a terrible fight here. We need your help."

<What help?> I asked suspiciously.

"We're trying to keep the *Veleek* distracted. It chases after morphing energy. It's drawn to anyone morphing. So we're morphing every five minutes or so, hoping to wear it out."

<How do you know it wears out?>

"We don't."

<This isn't much of a plan,> I said. <Are you Animorphs always this hopeless?>

"Pretty much," Cassie said ruefully. "The bad guys have all the power. Sometimes we think it's all a hopeless fight."

<A hopeless fight?> I asked. <Isn't that the best kind?>

Cassie laughed. "You may have lost your memory, but you're still Rachel. It's about time for me to morph. Let me jump off."

<No,> I said. <The beast couldn't lift me. I was too big. Stay on and morph where you are. It will come after us, but if it can't lift *me*, it may not be able to get *you*.>

I felt her pat the back of my massive head. "My girl, Rachel," she said affectionately. "Here goes nothing."

<What are you going to morph into?>

"Something small enough that maybe the dust beast won't be able to separate me from you. A squirrel."

<We can morph into small animals?>

"Sometimes smaller is better."

I felt a strange scraping, tickly feeling on my back, as the girl who said she was my friend became smaller.

CHAPTER 31
Marco

Aaaaaahhhhh! I thought, as the *Veleek* blazed after me.

"Huh huhh huhhhrrr hurrr HURRRHH!" I yelled.

I had a weird desire to pound my chest with my massive fists. But I stuck to my driving.

I heard the tornado behind me. I shot a look at the rearview mirror. The mirror was filled with gnashing mouths!

The truck was moving as fast as it could move.

Sudden flashes of brilliant red light. Coming from the sky. Dracon beams!

Then, in my headlights: an elephant!

WHAT?

I slammed on the brakes. Too late.

Sccrreeeeeeeech . . . WHAMPF!

Everything upside down. Rolling. Rolling. Pain. Suddenly flying!

Things hit me. Bushes ripped at me.

SLAM! I hit the ground hard. I was in a ditch half-filled with water. The truck was overturned on its back a few feet away. The wheels were still spinning. The headlights were still shining.

TSEEWW! TSEEEW! TSEEEW!

Dracon beams sliced the ground a few feet from my head. Bug fighters! I tried to move. Pain shot through my head. I moved my arms. They were still in one piece. If I had been in human form, I would have been killed. But it took more than a seventy-mile-an-hour crash to kill the gorilla.

From somewhere I heard an agonized trumpeting sound.

The dust beast was over me, a tornado of mouths and blades. But it didn't want me. It was after someone else.

I could feel consciousness dimming. I had to morph. Let it take me, if it had to.

Let it take me . . .

CHAPTER 32

Cassie

I felt myself shrink. Rachel's elephant back began to grow and grow, spreading out from me like some heaving, wobbling gray blanket.

A tail sprouted behind me. My face bulged out and grew pointed. Pale gray fur spread across my body.

I had morphed the squirrel before, of course. I knew what to expect. The body was wonderful. The senses keen and sharp. But the mind lived in a state of perpetual terror, always looking for predators. The only other emotion was hunger.

But I could control the squirrel's fear . . . if I could control my own.

Easier said than done. I was drawing the

monster to us. The energy that was allowing me to become a squirrel was bait to the dust beast.

Out of the corner of my eye, I saw headlights.

Something big was in the air behind the lights, a dark shadow that swallowed up the stars.

The beast! The *Veleek!*

I stopped the morph. I could feel my own fear. And if my fear met the squirrel's fear, I would never gain control.

Suddenly . . . PREDATOR!

The squirrel's terror shot through me.

Something overhead. Like a giant bird!

The squirrel's brain was screaming RUN! RUN! RUN!

TSEEEW! TSEEEW! TSEEEW!

Stabbing beams of brilliant light! Dracon beams. A Bug fighter coming in low above us.

I felt a surge as Rachel powered her huge body faster.

<What is happening?> Rachel cried in thought-speak.

But I was not morphed enough to use thought-speak. And my mouth was no longer fully human. The groaning sounds I made would mean nothing to Rachel.

TSEEEW!

Light so bright it blinded me!

"HhhrrrOOOOWWWuuhh!" Rachel screamed.

I smelled burned flesh. I blinked, trying to clear my half-human, half-squirrel eyes.

I saw a seared line of blackened flesh drawn down Rachel's side by a Dracon beam!

Headlights. Too close!

BAM!

I flew, tumbling through the air, a twisted, half-formed creature. I landed hard. But my fall was cushioned by dense bushes.

"HhhhRRRUUuuHHUUH!"

Through eyes half-human, half-squirrel, I saw a horrifying scene.

Rachel was on her side, trumpeting in pain and rage. A pickup truck lay on its back, wheels spinning. Just beyond the truck, a gorilla struggled to get up.

Marco!

A Bug fighter zipped overhead.

I stopped morphing. I froze. I was a two-foot-long creature with a tail and human hands and patchy gray fur poking through spandex and flesh.

The dust beast settled above us. It spread above the three of us — Rachel, Marco, and me. I looked up into that phalanx of gnashing teeth and whirring blades and eerie, staring eyes.

It would take whoever drew it by morphing.

It would take me . . . if I morphed.

And if I did nothing . . . if I just closed my eyes and hugged the dirt and did nothing . . .

The dream! Evil had come, to choose between me and another. Just like in the dream.

I heard the *Veleek*'s tornado roar. It had found its prey.

I closed my eyes.

CHAPTER 33

Ax

I watched it all in the wavering, shimmering hologram.

The elephant running. The truck racing, with the *Veleek* in hot pursuit.

The picture suddenly became much sharper. We were now seeing the scene through the gun camera of one of the Bug fighters.

A flashing light came on, an indicator that the Bug fighter was preparing to fire its Dracon beams.

Red beams lanced toward the elephant.

The elephant ran in terror. The truck hit. In a flash, it was all over. The elephant lay sprawled across the side of the road. The truck was overturned. The *Veleek* was hovering over the scene.

It dropped swiftly down, enveloping a ditch. It rose with something concealed inside it. The *Veleek* arced swiftly toward the sky, out of range of the Bug fighter's cameras.

<Come to me, my little pet,> Visser Three crowed. <Bring me my second Andalite bandit.> Visser Three turned his stalk eyes toward me. <You'll have company soon.>

I felt a sinking sensation. Who had the *Veleek* taken? Rachel? Cassie? Marco?

<Call the Bug fighters,> Visser Three said. <Tell them to land. Hold that large creature. The *Veleek* can't carry it until it demorphs into something smaller.>

"Visser . . ." one of the human-Controllers said timidly. "The Bug fighter has a crew of one Taxxon and one Hork-Bajir. May I suggest we contact some of our Earth-based human-Controllers? They will be less . . . ah, conspicuous . . . than Hork-Bajir."

<Do it,> Visser Three ordered. <But tell those Bug fighter crews they *will* contain that beast. They will not let it go. Or I'll see that they become the main course at the Taxxons' next meal. I'm going to my quarters. Call me when the *Veleek* arrives with my prize. Blank the Andalite's cage.>

My cage wall became opaque. I was alone again, unable to see out. I was left to imagine the fate of my human friends. I have never felt more worthless. More powerless.

I felt a sudden, sharp pain on my arm. What had Marco said they were? Fleas? I swatted it absentmindedly.

Wait!

A flea? Hadn't I heard Jake say he had done it? Yes. I was sure it was a flea. He had morphed a flea!

And he was, after all, just a human. Surely . . .

I reached for the flea. Easier said than done. It hopped away. I found it again. Again it escaped. On the third try, I caught it.

I squeezed the flea carefully between my fingers. I focused on the flea.

Yes! It might just work. We had very few animals that small on my own world. Perhaps the same was true of the Yeerks. The Visser would not expect me to morph something so tiny.

In which case, I might have one slim chance.

I had morphed a fly. And I had morphed an ant. But as small as they were, they were not small enough. An ant is far larger than a flea. Many times larger. But a flea is nearly invisible.

It was time to get very small. Time to morph.

I began to shrink at a startling rate.

Each morphing is unique. Things don't happen logically. Some parts of your body change in *shape* when they are still far too large in *size*.

Other times the parts of your body shrink down, becoming very tiny and only changing shape at the last minute.

This explains why, even as I was still a couple of feet tall, I suddenly felt two long tusks come shooting out of my mouth. Two long teeth. And I knew immediately what they were used for: These were what the flea used to pierce my skin and drink my blood.

Why a flea should have a taste for Andalite blood is a mystery. But now I knew *how* the little monster did his dirty work. And I really did not want to dwell on that image.

My legs and arms began to segment. Joints appeared where they should not have been. Primitive joints that scraped as I moved.

My tail withered away and my body swelled. I was bloating up. At the same time, my blue and tan fur gave way to an exoskeleton — a shell. I could hear my bones dissolving. I could feel sickening lurches as my internal organs all disappeared. My complex Andalite hearts became something that was barely a valve. Long, spiked hairs shot from my jointed legs. A sort of shell helmet fringed with backward-raked spikes replaced my face.

And all the while, the floor of my cage grew vastly wider. And closer and closer. I felt I was on an endless landscape of smooth black glass.

My stalk eyes went blind as they became short, stubby antennae. My sight in my main eyes dimmed and shattered into a thousand points of gray light.

I was almost blind. What I could see was nothing but shades of gray. Dots, not shapes.

I could not hear in the usual sense, but I could pick up subtle vibrations through my antennae and through all the hairs on my minuscule body.

I stood on my six invisibly small legs, protected by plates of shell armor. Almost blind. Almost unable to hear. Afraid.

The next move was up to the Yeerks.

I waited and ticked off the minutes. The flea's brain was scarcely a brain at all. It contained almost nothing. The sum total of what the flea "knew" was this: Jump toward warmth and the smell of life.

Since there was no warmth and no smell of life, the flea brain had nothing much to say.

I waited. And hoped. And feared. And listened for the Visser's thought-speech.

There are two kinds of thought-speech: open and closed. Open thought-speak can be "heard" by anyone. Closed thought-speak is like a human whispering to only one person. The Visser gave his orders in open thought-speak, so that everyone heard.

That was how I knew when he'd returned. From a distance I heard, <You and you. And you two. Follow me to the bridge.>

I tried to control the fear that welled up in me at his approach. I hated him. I knew I had to live on that hate and try not to let the fear overpower me. My time would come, I told myself. I would avenge Elfangor. I would save my honor.

<Where is the *Veleek*? Then open the hatch, you idiot, and let it in! Yes, right here on the bridge. And brighten the Andalite's cage. I want to see these old friends meet.>

I saw light, which was actually just an increase in the number of gray dots. There was a silence from Visser Three for about two seconds. Then an explosion of enraged thought-speech.

<FOOLS! Where is it? Where is it? I'll kill every one of you if it has escaped!>

Suddenly, a rush of air! I felt it waft across my bristles and antennae. Then, the scent of exhaled breath. A sensation of some warm object. The smells of a living creature!

<NO! Don't open the cage!> Visser Three yelled.

Too late, I thought. *JUMP!*

Above my back legs was a biological spring. It fired. The energy went to my legs and I went flying.

I've seen humans jump. They cannot jump

their own height. Even we Andalites can barely jump our own height. But the flea . . . well, the flea can jump a hundred times his own height. It was as if a human being could simply leap over a sixty-story building.

I flew through the air. And as I flew, I somersaulted over so that I was flying legs first.

I hit something and stopped very suddenly.

<Close the cage!> Visser Three screamed.

I felt a swift movement in the air just above me. The thing I was attached to fell.

And even as he fell, I could sense that he no longer smelled like life.

CHAPTER 34

Marco

Despite the fact we had kind of figured out that the dust creature wasn't actually trying to *eat* us, I was still slightly worried as it wrapped me up out of the ditch and carried me away.

"Slightly worried," as in crying like a baby.

I could feel that we were rising upward. But I was more concerned with just breathing, which was hard enough. The dust beast swirled around me, choking me, binding me, imprisoning me.

Suddenly, I sensed that we had stopped moving. A few moments later, the dust beast released me.

I don't know what I expected to see, but it sure wasn't this. I was on something that looked like the bridge of the starship *Enterprise*, only triangular. Instead of Data or Sulu or Worf or Spock, there were a bunch of Taxxons and a circle of Hork-Bajir with their weapons drawn. I also saw an open, empty box that looked like it could be a cage. And just in front of the box was a dead Hork-Bajir.

Finally — and this was the worst part — instead of either Captain Kirk or Captain Picard, there was Visser Three.

Visser Three, with Hork-Bajir blood on his tail. Visser Three, not looking happy. Not that he has probably ever looked happy, exactly.

Visser Three. The dust monster hovering above us, filling the top of the room like a storm cloud. Taxxons at computer screens. A circle of Hork-Bajir armed with Dracon beams.

And me, a gorilla, in the middle of all this.

It would have been funny. If it had been happening to someone else.

<Morph out of that stupid form,> Visser Three snapped.

I said nothing. We had faced Visser Three before. We never spoke, for fear he would be able to tell that we were human, not Andalite.

<Someone remove that garbage,> Visser Three said, pointing at the dead Hork-Bajir. <And find that Andalite! Bring in bio-scanners. He didn't disappear, he's just morphed something very small.>

Andalite? He had to mean Ax. Which meant Ax was still alive. And he had escaped! Which explained the poor Hork-Bajir. Visser Three is a hard guy to work for.

I felt a surge of hope. Ax was alive!

<Marco?> I jumped. Not far, because gorillas aren't big jumpers. I just sort of jerked in surprise. Every one of the Hork-Bajir tightened his grip on his weapon.

<Marco? Is that you? It's Ax.>

<Ax! It's me. Are you sure Visser Three can't "hear" us?>

<Just keep thought-speaking directly to me,> Ax said.

<Where are you?>

<I morphed a flea.>

<Good. Maybe you can get away then. You're practically invisible. I'm in gorilla morph. I'm kind of noticeable.>

<I have a plan.>

<Oh, good,> I said. <All our plans are working out so well. Where are you?>

<The safest place I could think of,> Ax said. <I'm on Visser Three.>

I stared at Visser Three. Somewhere in his Andalite fur, Ax was hiding. Visser Three glared at me.

<I told you to morph out of that ludicrous

shape,> Visser Three said to me. <Don't force me to use painful measures.>

<Did you hear that?> I asked Ax.

<Yes. He was thought-speaking openly. Don't morph. Don't say anything. Just tell me — do you see a computer console nearby? There will probably be a Taxxon working it.>

<I see a bunch of consoles. And a bunch of Taxxons. And Visser Three looking like he's ready to barbecue me.>

<Any console will do. Do you see a small square pad that the Taxxon is touching?>

<Yeah. All of the Taxxons are pressing one hand — if that's a hand — on these little squares.>

<Why do you defy me, Andalite?!> Visser Three demanded. <To what possible purpose? Sooner or later you have to emerge.>

<Those are interfaces,> Ax said. <Like your human keyboards. When you touch it, you can transmit commands directly to the computer. It's similar to thought-speech, however the basic scientific principle is actually —>

<Ax? I don't need a science lecture. Visser Three is looking at me like I'm his beef jerky, so if you have a plan, just do it!>

<Okay. Everything will go a bit crazy in a few minutes. Just go for the console. Press your hand

on it and think “open hatch.” Just think “open hatch.”>

<What are you going to do?>

Ax laughed. He seldom laughs. It surprised me.

<Heh-heh-heh. That *Veleek* goes after morph energy. So I’m going to give it some morph energy to go after.>

Visser Three was still staring at me. I could practically see the wheels turning in his evil brain. <Why? Why are you afraid to demorph? Why won’t you speak? The other Andalite spoke. Why don’t you?>

Then . . .

Over all our heads, the dust monster began to rotate. Faster. Faster.

“Visser *gullhadrash* is *muragg Veleek*!” a Hork-Bajir said in their weird mix of English and their own native tongue.

But Visser Three had already noticed. It would have been impossible not to. The *Veleek* was going totally tornado! A tornado with sharp teeth and slashing blades. Anything that wasn’t bolted down was flying around the bridge.

Suddenly ropes of dust shot down from the twirling cloud. Ropes that wrapped Visser Three up like a package!

I caught a glimpse of something on Visser

Three's back. It was a bug, growing slowly larger, already an inch long.

Ax!

The Hork-Bajir all leapt forward, trying instinctively to rescue the Visser from the dust creature.

Big mistake. The first Hork-Bajir tried to slash at the whirling dust cloud with his bladed arm. In a split second, he no longer had that arm.

"Aaaarrrggg!" The Hork-Bajir screamed.

This was my chance. I barreled toward the closest computer console. A Hork-Bajir, half-fixated on the dust monster and half on me, got in the way. I hit him full force with my head down like a charging bull.

The Hork-Bajir staggered back and splayed across a Taxxon. The Taxxon's weak legs collapsed. I didn't wait for them to get up. I punched a second Taxxon with my big gorilla fist. He scuttled back.

I was in the clear!

<Water!> Visser Three cried from within the swirling dust cloud. <Water!>

He was *thirsty*? At a time like this he was thirsty?

I pressed my hand on the computer console. *Open hatch,* I thought. *Open hatch. Right now.*

To my utter amazement, it worked.

I could barely see through the tattered edges of the dust monster's storm, but the ceiling of the bridge seemed to split down the middle. It began to open. I could see stars outside.

This was Ax's plan? To open the bridge up to the vacuum of space? We would all be sucked out instantly and die. I considered reversing the command. I wasn't ready to die.

But then I noticed something: We were not getting sucked out into space.

And then I noticed something else: a cloud. *Above* us. We were in the atmosphere!

<Fools!> Visser Three screamed. <They're trying to escape! Get him. Get him! Get that monkey!>

Monkey? *Monkey?* I'd show them monkey!

I turned. Six Hork-Bajir warriors advanced on me, their bladed wrists and elbows flashing.

<Ax? Um. . .I have the hatch open. And whatever you're planning on us doing next, now would be a very good time. Right now.>

CHAPTER 35

Ax

I morphed out slowly. I had no intention of going all the way. My plan depended on my remaining a flea.

As I began to morph, I could feel the air swirling wildly around me. It was working! My morphing had drawn the *Veleek.* It sensed the morphing energy and it was now doing what Visser Three had programmed it to do. It was capturing the morph.

Of course, in capturing me, it also captured the Visser.

I heard Visser Three yell for water. Why? What was the purpose of that?

Then, I heard Marco say, <Ax? Um . . . I have the hatch open. And whatever you're planning on

us doing next, now would be a very good time. Right now.>

I reversed morph. Back to total flea morph. The hairs on Visser Three's back, which had shrunk to the size of tall trees, now rose up again around me, taller than the tallest building.

I felt my flea armor-plate clank back into place. I was once again not much bigger than a comma on this page.

It was time to move. I released the massive spring power in my hind legs and fired myself away from the Visser's body. I hit a wall of wind.

I was caught in a swirling mass of dust. The particles were roughly my own size. They shot past me at incredible speed.

SLAM!

A particle hit me! It stuck to me. It was impaled on my own flea "combs," the spikes that protected the joints in my armor. It was stuck to me.

And only then, locked together with it, was I able to see it through my weak flea eyes. It was alive! It was a creature my own size, but with a hundred minuscule wings that beat the air. It had antennae, but different than any seen on Earth. These antennae were covered in tiny, upturned bowls. Like the dishes of primitive human radio telescopes. Those were the structures it used to sense energy sources.

There were no eyes. And no mouth. But two long filaments, like strands of wire, swept back from the front of the creature. These must be how it fed: by channeling the energy down the wires.

The *Veleek* was not one creature. It was billions! It was a swarm of billions of these tiny creatures. They had evolved into a swarm that could come together and become a destructive entity of gnashing teeth and slicing blades. But in reality they were separate insectlike creatures that fed on energy.

I motored my tiny front legs and shoved the *Veleek* away. Its wings beat, and in a flash it was gone.

Suddenly . . . a huge, silvery globule the size of a human house came shooting past. It hit several of the dust creatures and knocked them away. Then more. More!

A spinning globule hit me. It wrapped itself around me. I was trapped. Trapped, falling, falling!

A strange substance pressed all around me, enclosing me, smothering me.

Water!

The Yeerks had turned on a water hose! That's what Visser Three had been calling for. Water!

The drop of water that enclosed me splatted against the floor. I could not get away. It clung to me. It was like glue to my flea body.

Then . . . I was out! I was on dry ground. But water droplets loaded with powerless dust monsters were showering all around me like a meteor storm.

<Marco! Stamp your feet! I need to find you!>

<I'm a little busy,> Marco cried. <I got Hork-Bajir here looking for trouble! And someone turned on the sprinklers.>

<Stamp your feet!>

I felt a new vibration rumble through the floor. I knew where it was coming from. I leaped. I tumbled through the air. I landed in a forest of gigantic hairs, each as thick as the biggest tree.

<Where are you?> Marco yelled.

<On you!> I said. <We have to get out of here!>

<How?>

<Jump through the open hatch!>

<I'm a gorilla not a . . . wait! I have an idea!>

I felt a shuddering vibration like an earthquake that rolled through Marco's gorilla body. Then, movement. Then, wind whipping past at incredible speed.

<Where are we now?> I asked.

<The good news is, we're out of the ship. I used a couple Hork-Bajirs as a ladder and climbed over them! That's the good news.>

<You seem to be implying that there might be some bad news, too,> I said.

<Oh yeah,> Marco said. <The bad news is we're about two miles up in the air and we are plummeting to Earth.>

CHAPTER 36

Rachel

The truck hit my back right leg. It must have shattered the bone, because the pain was incredible.

The impact knocked me several feet. I fell and my head slammed the concrete.

Maybe that's what did it. I lay there on my side, breathing with difficulty. My eyes were closed.

FLASH! A construction site, late at night. The light in the sky was gone. Now it was in front of me, resting on the ground. A spaceship! It had landed. There was a voice in my head. It came from nowhere. No, it came from him? The alien! I could see him, lying there injured. The Yeerks. *The Yeerks,* he said.

They have come to destroy you.

FLASH! A barn full of animals in cages. Birds. Foxes. Squirrels. Raccoons. Bats. And Cassie was there.

Yes, Cassie. My friend.

And the others. I could *see* them now. They had been with me at the construction site. And ever since that night we had been joined together.

Animorphs. That was the word. It was Marco's word.

FLASH! I was flying. I was flying on wings that seemed to stretch forever. Soaring high on the thermals. An eagle, that's what I was — a bald eagle.

Then . . . yes! They had swarmed me. A bunch of smaller blackbirds. They had swarmed me, and I had hit the tree and then . . .

<Rachel! It took Marco!>

I opened my elephant eyes. A squirrel stood nervous and jumpy, tail twitching, mouth working almost as if it were talking.

<Cassie,> I said.

<It took Marco,> Cassie said again. <It took Marco and I didn't do anything.>

<Marco. I remember Marco.>

<You do? Is your memory coming back?>

<Yeah. Mostly. It still feels shaky.>

Over our heads swooped two Bug fighters.

Bug fighters. The words were right there in my brain! I knew what they were. Bug fighters. Crew: one Hork-Bajir, one Taxxon. I could form mental pictures of the Hork-Bajir. The Taxxon was still hazy.

But both were Yeerks. That was the important thing. Each had a Yeerk in its head.

<I can't stand up,> I told Cassie. <The elephant's leg is broken. I'm morphing back to human.>

<Me, too. It's gone for now. The *Veleek* is gone,> Cassie said. <Rachel, I should have morphed while the dust beast was here. I could have drawn it away from Marco. I was scared.>

<Of course you were scared. So was I,> I said. I could feel myself shrinking. My legs, as big as telephone poles, were becoming normal human legs. The tusks sucked back into my mouth and split to form front teeth. The trunk grew weak, lost its muscles, and shriveled back to form my nose and mouth.

"Why didn't the dust beast attack us?" I wondered, as soon as my mouth could form speech.

"It's off, carrying Marco away. Maybe killing him," Cassie wailed. "I should have —"

"Look, Cassie," I said sharply. "That's what happened, all right? It's in the past. We have the present to worry about." I pointed to the two Bug fighters that had looped around overhead and were coming back toward us at a much slower speed.

"Cassie, I don't remember," I said. "Can we morph again so quickly?"

"Yes. Yes, we can. It's exhausting though. But we don't have a choice. We can't let them catch us in human morph. It would blow our cover forever!"

"Cassie, we need morphs that can move fast and I don't remember everything we have available," I said urgently.

Cassie concentrated. "It's night. The woods. Let's go airborne. We've both acquired owl morphs. We used them to guard Jake when he was taken by the Yeerk. Great horned owls."

I squeezed my eyes shut. An owl? I had morphed an owl? Yes. Yes, I remembered. I could *feel* it.

The Bug fighters took up positions, hovering in the air just a hundred yards to either side of us. In the distance I heard sirens screaming in the night — police cars growing closer. Probably Controllers, not *real* policemen.

I focused all my thoughts on making the change. I squeezed my eyes shut and concentrated. When I opened my eyes again, it was broad daylight.

No. Not daylight. I was seeing the world through the eyes of the owl. It might as well have been noon. I could see everything! I could see every detail of the Bug fighters. I could see deep into the black woods. I could see the flashing blue lights of the police cars as if they were right in my face.

<Ready?> Cassie asked.

<Yeah. I think so.>

<Follow me,> Cassie said. She flapped her wings. I flapped mine. We flew, just a foot off the ground.

Suddenly, a large creature dropped from the hovering Bug fighter. It dropped more than fifty feet, hit the ground, rolled, and was up! My owl vision saw him as if he were bathed in a spotlight.

<Hork-Bajir!> I yelled. <Straight ahead.>

A second later, another Hork-Bajir dropped from above. With amazing speed, they were up and running for us. Their arm blades glinted in the moonlight.

We were flying straight at them. Too low! Too low, and not enough time to get off the ground! If we turned, we would lose altitude. They would get us before we could get clear.

<Straight at them,> I said.

<My girl, Rachel,> Cassie said grimly. Then, <Go for the eyes!>

I flapped my wings with desperate energy. I raked my talons forward. The Hork-Bajir came straight at us. We went straight for them. I knew right then that my fate was not in my own hands anymore. If their orders were to kill us, we would die. I could measure the distance, I knew my own speed, and I could see the superhuman speed of the Hork-Bajir, with their flashing, bladed arms.

RRRROOOOAAAWWWRRR!

Something big flew through the air. I saw a flash of orange and black. My Hork-Bajir went down hard with a huge tiger on his back, slamming him down into the dirt. The Hork-Bajir in front of Cassie turned to see, for just a split second.

Cassie blew past him.

The tiger leaped back off the downed Hork-Bajir.

I sailed above them all, flapping for dear life.

<Let's get outta here!> Jake said.

<Definitely,> I agreed.

<What about Marco?> Jake asked. <Have you seen Marco?>

CHAPTER 37

Marco

<Aaaaaaaaahhhhhhh!>

I don't think in the entire history of planet Earth that any gorilla has ever plummeted through the night from a height of two miles. So it was a first for "both" of us.

I was spinning wildly, down, down, down through the cold night air. Far below me . . . way too far below me . . . I saw streetlights. And car lights. And neon store lights. And right beside me, almost all around me, clouds.

I was a four-hundred-pound gorilla who had just decided to go skydiving without a parachute.

<Aaaaaaahhhhhhh!>

<Marco, why are you screaming? It hurts my head.>

<We're gonna die, you alien lunatic!>

<No, we won't die. Don't be foolish,> Ax said.

<Maybe *you* won't. You're a flea! You'll bounce. I'll hit the ground like rock!>

<Marco, morph into a bird.>

<Oh. Duh,> I said, feeling a little foolish. <Is there time?>

<I don't know. Maybe we should hurry,> Ax said in his annoyingly calm Andalite way.

Now, the problem we had was a simple one: You can't morph from one animal into another. You have to return to your natural form first. So I had to become human. Then I could morph into a bird.

A minute later we were no longer a gorilla and a flea falling. Now we were a human and an Andalite falling.

And now the ground was no longer way too far below us. Now it was way too close!

"Aaaaaaahhhhh!" I yelled.

<Aaaaaahhhhhh!> Ax screamed in thought-speak.

I felt relieved that at least he was screaming now, too. But mostly I was busy noticing that I could make out individual houses, ringed by faint light. I could see individual car headlights and taillights. And I could see the mall parking lot, which was almost empty except for a crew painting new stripes on the blacktop.

"Aaaaaaahhhhhh!"

I focused as hard as I could. I had long ago morphed an osprey. That's a type of hawk. It's mostly dark gray-brown, with a sort of mottled white underside and a dark beak. It's a cool bird. But you know what? Right at that moment, I didn't care what kind of bird I became, as long as it had wings.

"Grow, wings, GROW!" I yelled, and the wind screaming past my face blew the words right out of my mouth.

Feathers began to form on my skin. I felt myself shrink. I felt my bones grow light, hollow. I could hear a grinding sound as the bones of my skull scrunched down to hold a much smaller brain.

Too slow. Way too slow.

I could see people now. The guys working in the mall parking lot. I could see people! And I was still falling.

No way I could morph in time!

No time! The ground!

It was going to hit me! It was jumping up to hit me! I could see one of the work crew look up at me.

I could see his eyes!

I spread my arms wide.

No! Not arms. WINGS! WIIINNNGGS!

SWOOOOOOSH! The wind snapped my wings

back, straining every muscle, and I blew at ninety miles an hour, just inches off the freshly painted blacktop.

<Yah-HAH!> I yelled. I glanced left. Ax was right beside me, in his own harrier morph.

<That was exciting,> Ax said.

<Yes, it was. Let's never, *ever* do that again.>

<Ever,> Ax agreed.

CHAPTER 38

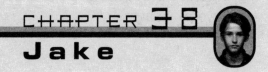

Jake

We spent a bad night, Cassie and Rachel and I. Cassie and I went to our homes. Rachel spent the night at Cassie's house, because otherwise she'd have had to explain to her mom why she wasn't at gymnastics camp.

Rachel was still shaky, but her memory was almost all the way back to normal. I figured the best thing for her would be to spend some time with Cassie.

As for me, I dragged home at almost midnight. There was no question: I was grounded. I didn't even argue. No TV. No Sega. Inside the house by five o'clock. Wash all dishes. Take out all trash. For two weeks. And oh, by the way, clean out the garage.

I didn't say anything but "Yes, sir," and, "Yes, ma'am," and, "I'm really sorry I worried you."

Then I went up to my room and tried not to imagine what Visser Three was doing to Ax and Marco.

I've never felt so tired and so bad. I fell asleep in my clothes, facedown on my unmade bed.

We were beaten. That's what I fell asleep thinking. We were done. The dust monster would be back. We had survived — most of us — but we would never be able to morph safely. We Animorphs were finished. The battle was done. Nothing now stood between the Yeerks and complete control of Earth.

And you know what? That thought just made me feel relieved. I was too tired to fight . . . too tired.

The next thing I knew . . .

"Booga booga booga boooga!"

"Whaaaa?!"

I sat up, spun around, twisting myself up in my sheets, then promptly fell out of my bed.

Marco laughed so hard he started crying.

"How did you get here?" I demanded. Then, "You're alive?"

"No, I am the ghost of Marco. Fear me!"

"What time is it?"

"Like ten in the morning," Marco said. He went to the window and opened the blinds.

I recoiled from the bright sunlight. "Cassie said the *Veleek* carried you away."

"Yes, it did. And now we're going steady. Look, get with it. Wake up, fearless leader. We're all alive, and waiting for you to come and lead the counterattack."

"Counterattack?" I glanced at the door.

"Don't worry," Marco said. "Tom's out. I checked."

"I can't go anywhere," I said. "I'm so busted for coming in late."

"Um . . . yeah. I talked to your dad on my way up. He mentioned that little fact. He said if you clean the garage you can go out for a while. It seemed very important to him. Like maybe if you cleaned the garage he would be the happiest guy in the world."

"Sure. Why not? My mom has been after him for a month to clean the garage. So now he gets to dump it off on me. Why wouldn't he be happy? You going to help me?"

"Me? Help clean the garage? As if."

I smiled. "I'm glad you're not dead, Marco."

"Me, too."

"Get everyone together. Give me three hours to deal with the garage. We'll meet at the edge of the woods. No one morphs. Got that? *No one* morphs."

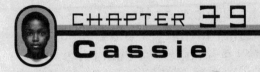

CHAPTER 39
Cassie

<I can't believe you guys were doing all this while I was sleeping!> Tobias raged. <Playing tag with some dust monster from Saturn? Rachel having amnesia till Marco plowed into her with a truck? Escaping from Visser Three's Blade ship? And I'm sleeping the entire time? No way! I missed all the fun.>

"You're the only one who can't morph," Jake said matter-of-factly. "So the *Veleek* isn't interested. Lucky you."

"It's the morphing that this *Veleek* goes after," Marco said, grinning his taunting grin. "It — or they, I should say — eat energy. It's not interested in your deep-fried hawk legs."

<Come stand over here, Marco,> Tobias said. <Stand under my branch.>

Everyone laughed. Except me. I hadn't slept much. It wasn't the dream this time. It was the memory. The dream had become real. And what sleep I had was broken by images of myself, scared and shivering while the *Veleek* hovered above us and finally dove on Marco.

I didn't like that memory. I don't mind being scared. We're all scared. But I didn't like knowing that I had kept myself safe at Marco's expense. There was only one word for a person who would do that: coward.

I didn't like that word. It twisted inside me.

"Okay, here's what we know," Jake said. "One: The *Veleek* is sort of an insect swarm. The individual particles spread out till they sense a type of energy they can eat, then they call the swarm together. The swarm forms into this beast that chews through anything. Two: Visser Three has altered this creature to serve his own purpose."

<Yes,> Ax said. <It is fairly simple, really. The Yeerks reprogrammed the beast to *hunt* for morph energy, but to *eat* a different kind of energy: the power of their spacecraft engines.>

Rachel nodded. "Like a trained hunting dog. A hunting dog chases the fox or whatever, but only because its master will give it food of a different kind. The *Veleek* chased morph energy, brought the morph to its master, then was rewarded with energy from the ships."

"Exactly," Jake said. "The *Veleek* is Visser Three's dog. And unfortunately, it is awesome. Maybe unbeatable."

"No," I said quietly. "Not unbeatable. It couldn't lift Rachel when she was in elephant mode. She was too heavy. It has limits. Also, on board the Blade ship the Yeerks used water to control the *Veleek*."

Everyone was looking at me now.

Jake said, "So, what do we do with this information?"

"I . . . I have a plan," I said. I took a deep breath. "But I have one condition: I have to be the one who does it."

I told them my plan.

"Cassie, this is beyond dangerous," Jake said when I was done. "Why should *you* do it?"

"Because." I looked at Marco and met his gaze. "I let the *Veleek* take Marco. I could have morphed. I could have drawn it to me. I let it take Marco."

Marco smiled wryly. "Cassie, it's no big deal. Here I am, fine and healthy. And as cute as ever."

"That's not the point," I said. "I was a coward."

Rachel rolled her eyes. "Good grief! Cassie, you have been in every fight we've been in. You are the farthest thing in the world from being a coward!"

"Easy for you to say, *Xena: Warrior Princess.*"

"What?"

"Don't you remember? That's what Marco calls you."

Rachel made a face. "I guess there are still one or two holes in my memory." She looked suspiciously at Marco. "Do I like it when you call me that? Or do I kick your butt?"

"Nice try, Rachel. But you can't distract me. I'm doing this," I said flatly. "It's my plan. I'm doing it."

"Cassie," Jake said, pleading with his eyes.

I took his hand in mine and gave it a squeeze. "You know it's a good plan, Jake. And you know I'm the person to do it. It's a new morph, with no chance to try it out first. And I'm the best morpher."

No one said anything. I could see worry in Jake's eyes. Rachel put her hand on my shoulder.

"All right," Jake said heavily. "Let's go to the beach."

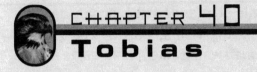

CHAPTER 40
Tobias

I caught a beautiful thermal rising up from the cliffs along the ocean. Just perfect! I spread my wings and felt the warm updraft grab me. It was like being fired out of a slingshot. I rose and rose and circled high above the ocean. I needed all the altitude I could get.

I could not believe that Cassie felt like the weak link in our group. I mean, I was the one who had slept through half of what happened! It was embarrassing. It was frustrating.

The only good thing was that at least I had a role to play in Cassie's plan.

Normally a red-tailed hawk is not a water bird. We don't fly that well over water, because over water you don't get thermals. But I was way,

way up, and with a little luck I could stay aloft long enough to find what I was looking for.

I headed out to sea. And as soon as I was well out over the gray-blue water, I felt the air grow slack. I worked the headwind to compensate, though, and I was able to hang on to most of my altitude.

All the while, I scanned the ocean beneath me. I have amazing vision, but it isn't adapted for seeing *through* water, like a bald eagle's or an osprey's is. Still, if what I was searching for was down there, I'd see it well enough.

I was getting tired by the time I spotted the spout. It was actually back, closer to shore than I was flying. That was lucky.

I turned south a bit, and veered at an angle that brought me nearer to shore, though still more than two miles out from the beach.

And then, it was just below me. I could see it plowing majestically through the waves. It rose and blew out its lungs, then dove again. It reappeared a hundred yards farther south. Always south.

I wheeled to my left and headed back toward shore. I was tired, and glad to see land. But I wouldn't get much of a chance to rest. The real test was still ahead.

With my hawk's eyes I swept the beach below.

It was not crowded, but still, it took a few minutes to find them.

I spilled air and dropped down to meet my friends.

<I have one for you, Cassie,> I said. <I found a whale.>

CHAPTER 41
Cassie

"I'm just saying there are people who *should* be lying out on the beach, and there are people who *shouldn't* be," Marco said. "Do you see fat hairy old guys in Speedos on *Baywatch*? No. No. On *Baywatch* they have a law against it. David Hasselhoff kicks anybody off the beach who isn't good-looking. We need the Hasselhoff law here. That's all I'm saying."

"So you wouldn't mind never going to the beach, Marco?" Rachel said wanly, not really interested in playing put-down games with Marco.

We walked along the beach, pretending everything was normal. Pretending we weren't worried. Pretending everything was fine.

Rachel was still quiet. I think the experience

of losing her memory had shaken her up. Rachel is someone who is always in control. She's very brave at dealing with threats. But this was something new to her: a threat that had come from inside.

Marco was trying too hard to tell jokes and make everyone relax. He felt somehow he was responsible for my feeling bad. He wanted to tell me that he didn't blame me. But he'd already told me, and I'd said thanks and still I felt bad. Marco didn't know how to deal with that. So he tried to make everyone laugh.

Jake was just one big tension machine. He hides it well, but I know him. I know when he's upset. It's something you see in the way he presses his lips together a little too hard. And a certain hooded look in his eyes.

And then . . . Tobias was back.

<I have one for you, Cassie,> he said. <I found a whale.>

I waved at him. Tobias told us where the whale was.

Jake stopped walking. "You don't have to do this, Cassie. The force of the impact . . . if you hit too fast . . . besides, maybe the *Veleek* isn't even around anymore . . ."

I couldn't look him in the eye. He was offering me an easy way out. I didn't want to be tempted.

"I'm going in," I said as calmly as I could.

"I could do this, Cassie," Rachel said.

"Do three morphs, six changes, including one that's totally new, all that quickly?" I asked her. "You all say I'm the fastest morpher. The one who gets control over a new morph easiest. I'm the person for this job."

To my surprise, Jake nodded. "Cassie's right. It's her job." He took my hand. "But we'll be there for you."

The four of us walked into the surf. Ax had to sit this one out. He would have had to morph back to his original form, and that probably wouldn't have gone over too well at the beach. We had chosen a spot far from the lifeguards. We didn't want someone deciding we needed to be rescued.

I splashed into the cold surf. Water bubbled around my ankles, then my legs, my waist. I plunged forward and swam away from shore. The others were right beside me. Tobias had flown to the top of the cliff to rest up for a few seconds.

I swam out to sea, and as I swam, I focused on the first morph. Some morphs are terrifying. Some are disgusting. Some overwhelm you with their animal instincts of fear and hunger. Other morphs make you feel invincible with their power.

And some morphs . . . not many, but a few, are simply wonderful.

As I swam, I felt my face bulge out and out and out. I felt my legs begin to fuse together. I felt my skin become thick and rubbery. I could even feel when my lungs shut down for a moment, and a second later were sucking air from a hole behind my head.

From far off, I heard Tobias's thought-speak, faint but understandable.

<It's coming! The *Veleek*! It's coming!>

I was a creature with feet but no legs, hands that were flat and gray, and no arms. I had human eyes that still stung from the salt water, but a blowhole in the back of my neck. I was half-human, half-bottlenose dolphin.

I rolled onto my side to look upward. And there it was: Visser Three's hunting dog. The *Veleek*. The dust monster. A tornado of energy-hungry particles that swirled like a small tornado.

I dove beneath the waves. And when I surfaced, it was still there. But it had not come closer.

<It doesn't like the water,> Marco said.

<I guess not,> I agreed.

<You were right, Cassie,> Rachel said.

<Let's hope so.>

I felt the last of the changes as I became a true dolphin. The joy! I had forgotten how happy the dolphin was. It seemed strange, given what we were up against.

But still, with all our worry, the dolphin joy was hard to contain.

<Let's go find this whale!> Rachel said.

We took off at full dolphin speed. I fired a series of clicks from the organ in my head. The clicks resounded through the water, and came back to me in echoes. The echoes painted a picture of what was in the water around me.

<I have him on echolocation,> I told the others.

<Yeah,> Jake agreed. <A little left. Not far now.>

Soon I could hear the whale crashing through the water. We raced up alongside him, faster than he was, but insignificant beside his huge bulk.

It was like running next to a truck or a train. His flank was a gray wall, scarred and dotted with crusts of barnacles.

Little ones, the whale said in a voice that was not a voice, in words that were not really words at all. *Strange cloud above*.

He kept moving, not really caring whether we were there or not. The *Veleek* kept pace above us, not able to attack, but not drawn off, either.

<Okay, guys. It's time,> I said. <Get ready.>

I began to demorph. Easier said than done. I was moving at whale speed, much faster than I could swim as a human.

Great one, do not dive, I asked the whale. Whether he heard me or understood me, let alone agreed, I could not say. It's hard to describe the way a whale communicates. The dolphins can hear their thought-speech, but it isn't words, really. More like strange, beautiful pictures that simply appear in your mind.

Jake and Rachel each sidled up next to me. They pressed their snouts against me, and pushed me through the water. I demorphed, and slowly my dolphin tail split to become legs. My flippers sliced into fingers.

I was fully human again and gasping for breath, with my face just out of the water. Just two feet off the water, the *Veleek* hovered — hungry, waiting for a chance.

I pressed my human hands against the side of the whale. I focused my mind on the process of "acquiring." It felt . . . wrong, somehow. As if I should have asked the whale's permission. But the slow, vague communication of whales does not allow for explanations. I needed his DNA.

He slowed and almost stopped. It was the acquiring trance. All animals become calm while they are being acquired. But it was hard to think of the whale as being just an animal. I had dealt with whales before. They are not intelligent in the same way humans are, but they have minds, and, I believe, souls.

When I was done acquiring the great one's DNA, I took my hands from him.

"I'm done!" I said, getting a mouthful of salt water.

My friends slowed down and the whale pulled away.

Now I was one of the most awkward things in the world: a human being in the ocean. I didn't fear drowning, because my friends were all around me in dolphin morph. But with the *Veleek* hanging above us, like a low ceiling of gnashing teeth, it was creepy.

"Is Tobias ready?" I asked.

<He's up above the *Veleek*,> Jake said. <How are you holding up?>

"So far — *glublub* — *pah! Pah!*" I spit salt water out of my mouth. "So far so good. I'm ready."

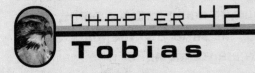

CHAPTER 42
Tobias

It was not my favorite kind of flying. Hawks are not like geese. We can't just power-fly, hour after hour. Personally, I don't know how geese do it.

A hawk likes a bit of a headwind to get lift for the takeoff. I had that, at least. But most of the time we hunt from trees, swooping down on unwary mice or rabbits. We don't go for serious altitude unless we can get some free lift from a thermal.

Otherwise it's hard work, flapping and flapping for altitude.

But I couldn't complain. Cassie had a worse job.

She rode my back in cockroach morph. She'd

had to finish the morph while literally underwater to keep away from the *Veleek.* She had morphed from human to dolphin to human to cockroach already. And more was coming.

<Hanging in there?> I asked her.

<Yeah. I'm fine. Is the *Veleek* following us?>

<No, the others are keeping it distracted down below. They're doing partial morphs, keeping it down near the surface of the water.>

<Good. How are you doing?>

<No problem,> I said. It was a lie. I was straining for every foot of altitude I could get, and I was wearing out. I had to get as high up as possible. Cassie would need every foot I could give her.

We were making progress. At about a hundred feet, I caught a nice gust of wind that I rode up to a thousand feet or so. But then it was dead air for a while. Totally dead air, and I was struggling.

<Tobias?>

<Yeah, Cassie.>

<Think this will work?>

<If I get you enough altitude, it will work.>

<Are you ever afraid?> she asked me.

<Who, me? I'm afraid of everything. I know I'm a predator and all, but do you know how many predators I have after me? Every golden eagle, every falcon. You know how fast they are? It's like getting hit by a bullet. They make me look

like the Goodyear blimp. Then there are the raccoons and foxes and snakes and even the occasional nervy house cat. And that's just the natural environment. Add to that the Yeerks, and the fact that I wake up sometimes and don't remember exactly what I am, boy or bird . . . yeah, Cassie, I'm afraid a lot of the time.>

<How do you handle it?>

<Who says I handle it? There's only one way to deal with fear: Be afraid. Be afraid, and then go ahead and do what you have to do, anyway.>

<Yeah. I guess that's true. Listen, Tobias, if I don't make it . . .>

<Oh, shut up. You're *going* to make it.>

<If I don't . . . if I don't, you know, then tell Jake that someday he has to tell my parents, okay? Someday, if it's ever safe. Tell them what happened to me. Promise?>

<Sure, Cassie. I promise.>

<Just don't tell my dad what happened to his truck,> she added, forcing a brave laugh. <He thinks it was stolen. We'd better leave it at that.>

<Cassie? This is it, kid. I can't go any higher.>

<Okay, Tobias. Thanks for the ride.>

I felt her scuttle down along my wing. And a second later I saw her falling, spinning. A girl who had become a cockroach, now falling from a mile up, trying to draw a monster to attack her.

A girl who thought she was a coward. It's

amazing how people can just not know themselves at all.

With my hawk eyes I saw her grow and grow, as human DNA reasserted itself.

And I saw the *Veleek* turn its many mouths toward the sky.

CHAPTER 43
Cassie

I fell. Almost blind, with roach's eyes, I fell.

I focused my mind on one thing: morphing. No time to wonder where the ocean surface was. No time to worry about the *Veleek*. Morph. Morph. Morph.

Hands. Legs. Arms. Eyes.

Eyes!

I could see! Below me, as far as I could see in every direction, water. Tiny white-peaked waves. Ripples that caught the sunlight. It was beautiful. Blue sky above. Blue water below. Water that would be as hard as concrete if I hit it too fast.

I could see Tobias circling above. And in the water below, the tiny pale-gray cylinders of Jake and Rachel and Marco.

And then, coming up to meet me like a tornado: the *Veleek*. It had sensed the morphing energy from my transformation back to human.

Was I fully human? Yes. I must be, because the exhaustion that hit me in a wave made my eyes flutter and my limbs go weak.

Too many morphs. Too quickly. And now . . .

Morph! Morph! Morph! I ordered myself. *Focus! Concentrate! Believe!*

But the changes were slow. So slow.

I focused my mind. But I was so tired. And it was so easy to just fall and fall and fall.

Morph, Cassie! Do it!

I felt changes. I felt myself growing . . .

And then, it was on me! The *Veleek* fired ropes of dust at me. They wrapped around me like the tentacles of an octopus. Wrapping around my hands that had become flippers. Around my legs that were melting together.

Ignore it! Morph! It's the only hope.

I felt the *Veleek* taking my weight. My momentum was slowing, but we were still dropping, me and the *Veleek* together.

Through the dust storm I caught a glimpse of the ocean below me. The cigar shapes of my friends were too large. Too close!

Morph, Cassie. One more time. Morph.

But I didn't have the strength. I was beaten. And then . . . at that moment, I felt the edge of the whale's brain brushing against mine. Its instincts, its DNA memories.

Help me, I pleaded.

In a dream of falling and falling, I reached out to a dark, vast being that I could not define. I reached out for the whale's strength.

Morph! Finish the morph!

Finish it, and then you can rest.

CHAPTER 44

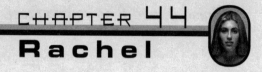

Rachel

At first I couldn't see her. But then, the cockroach grew and became larger. I could see her as a dot, way, way up in the sky.

<Here she comes,> I said.

The *Veleek* shuddered, sensing this new prey.

<Should we try to keep the *Veleek* interested any longer?> I asked.

<No,> Jake said. <It's up to Cassie now.>

Someday Jake will be a general or a president. He has that ability to make hard decisions, even about people he cares for.

She fell and grew, and became human again.

<She's too close! Not enough time!> I yelled.

<The *Veleek.* It will slow her down!> Marco said.

None of us had ever done so many morphs in such a short time. It was mind-boggling. It was impossible.

And yet, as the *Veleek* wrapped itself around her, she was already sprouting the flukes of a humpback whale.

Now all we could see was the *Veleek.* The dust storm wrapped around Cassie. It slowed. It slowed. And then . . .

<Am I crazy, or is it falling faster?> Marco asked.

<Yes, and YES!> I cried.

<She did it!>

Like a rock, the *Veleek* fell. Faster. Faster. It could not support the growing weight. It had not been able to lift an elephant, and what it was holding now was so much bigger.

It was wrapped around a full-grown humpback whale.

And it was falling toward the ocean.

At the last second, the *Veleek* tried to break free. But it had wrapped itself too tightly around the prey that was no longer prey.

I dove beneath the surface, just in time to witness . . .

Spuh-LOOOOOOSSSSHHH!

The tornado hit the water. All the billions of particles slammed into the ocean waves. In a split second, it was gone. Washed away.

And exploding away from the doomed *Veleek*, emerging from the wasted tornado, was a huge, sleek creature that depth-charged fifty feet straight down.

<Cassie! Cassie! Cassie! Are you all right?>

There was no answer. The whale fell through the water.

<Cassie! Answer me!>

And then there came a kick from that massive whale tail.

<Hah HAH!> Cassie yelled. <Take that, you big bag of wind!>

Cassie power-kicked her way to the surface and shot clear out of the water.

<Hey, Visser Three!> Cassie crowed. <I washed your dog for you!>

She fell back with a mighty splash. And we raced to join her.

<Good job, Cassie!> Jake said. <Scratch one *Veleek*.>

<I can't believe it,> Marco said. <We actually won one. We won. We flat out kicked butt.>

<Cassie, you must be exhausted,> Tobias said, swooping low and slow above us.

<Not anymore,> Cassie said. <I feel great. I thought we were beat. And guess what? We aren't. Not yet. Not by a long shot.>

Then, to my total amazement, she began to sing the deep, strange, haunting song of the humpback. The sound waves thrilled me, I don't quite know why.

<What are you singing?> Jake asked her. <What are the words?>

<It isn't words, exactly,> Cassie said. <But if it were, it would be just one word: hope.>

Don't miss

ANIMORPHS®

#8 The Alien

I morphed as quickly as I could, while being careful not to fall over as my third and fourth legs disappeared. At last, I stood on just two legs. It's both frightening and exciting. I mean, there you are, tottering back and forth with nothing to hold you up. Your feet can't grip, and they are too short to be much help in balancing.

All you can do if you start to fall is stand on one leg while you throw the second leg out to catch yourself. It's very unreliable. I don't know why humans evolved this way. They are the only species on this planet to walk around on just two legs, without wings or a tail to hold them up.

And I've certainly never heard of any other intelligent species trying to walk this way.

"Hey, grab him," Jake yelled as I began to lean back.

"Got him," Cassie said. She helped support me as I finished the morph.

Last of all the mouth appeared, a horizontal split in my face.

"Are you done?" Jake asked me.

"Yes. I am fully human." The sound delighted me. It's an amazing talent, this ability to make complex sounds. "Human. Mun. Hyew-mun. Human. Huh-yew-mun."

"Um, Ax? Don't do that, okay?" Jake said.

"What? What-tuh?"

"That. Where you play with every sound like it's a new toy."

"Yes, my prince. Not a toy. Toy! Toytoytoy-toy . . . . Sorry."

"This should be interesting," Cassie said, looking at Prince Jake.

Tobias came swooping low and rested on a tree branch. <It's kind of sweet,> he said. <Ax's first day of school.>

"His *only* day of school," Prince Jake said quickly. "This is just so he can learn how to be a more believable human. One time."

Prince Jake held up a single finger, indicating the number one.

"Yes, that is one," I agreed. "Now, let's go to school. I am looking forward to it. To it. Tewit."

"Remember, you're my cousin Phillip, from out of state."

"Phillip," I repeated confidently. "Phillip. Lip. Philup. Pah."

I like the sound the human letter "p" makes.

I set off toward the squat building that was the schoolhouse.

<Have fun,> Tobias said. He sounded just a little wistful in my mind. It was a strange thing, I guess. I, an alien, could go to his school. But he could not.

"I will," I called back over my shoulder.

Unfortunately, bending that way made me fall over. It takes practice to walk on just two legs.

COMING IN JUNE

He's a cross between a deer, a scorpion, and a human. But is this Andalite prepared to fight?

ANIMORPHS™

"Are you done?" Prince Jake asked me.

I considered. I was standing precariously on two legs. I possessed two strong arms and ten strong fingers. I was mostly without fur. My eyes were weak and totally unable to see anything except what was in front of me. My hearing was good. My mind was functioning normally.

And I had a mouth. "Yes," I said, using my mouth. "Yessss. Sssss. Yes-suh. I am in human morph."

I had morphed into a human.

ANIMORPHS #8: THE ALIEN

K.A. Applegate

COVER SHOWS AN ALIEN MORPH!

Visit the Web Site at: http://Scholastic.com/animorphs